China

The Whole Enchilada

by Mark Brown

Additional Music and Arrangements by

Paul Mirkovich

A SAMUEL FRENCH ACTING EDITION

SAMUEL FRENCH

FOUNDED 1830

NEW YORK HOLLYWOOD LONDON TORONTO

SAMUELFRENCH.COM

ISBN 978-0-573-66315-4   Printed in U.S.A.   #6292

**IMPORTANT BILLING AND CREDIT
REQUIREMENTS**

All producers of *CHINA – THE WHOLE ENCHILADA must* give credit to the Author of the Play in all programs distributed in connection with performances of the Play, and in all instances in which the title of the Play appears for the purposes of advertising, publicizing or otherwise exploiting the Play and/or a production. The name of the Author *must* appear on a separate line on which no other name appears, immediately following the title and *must* appear in size of type not less than fifty percent of the size of the title type.

In addition the following credit *must* be given in all programs and publicity information distributed in association with this piece:

China – The Whole Enchilada was originally produced as a Workshop Production of PlayFest! The Harriett Lake Festival of New Plays at the Orlando Shakespeare Theater in Partnership with UCF.

China - The Whole Enchilada was presented by THE NEW YORK INTERNATIONAL FRINGE FESTIVAL, a production of THE PRESENT COMPANY

CHINA – THE WHOLE ENCHILADA's world premiere was presented at the New York International Fringe Festival by The Present Company on August 8, 2008. The artists were as follows:

CAST:

PHILIP. . . . . Philip Nolen
ERIC . . . . .Eric Hissom
BRAD. . . . . Brad DePlanche

STAFF:

Director . . . . Jim Helsinger
Costume Designer . . . . Lisa Zinni
Scenic Consultants. . . . . .Joseph Fletcher, Thu Nguyen
Props. . . . . .Melissa A. Nathan
Graphic Designer. . . . . Thu Nguyen
General Manager. . . . . .Bailie Slevin
Production Stage Manager . . . . Kat West
Assistant Stage Managers. . . . . .Melissa A. Nathan
Assistant Director/Assistant Stage Manager . . . . .Joseph Fletcher
Press and Marketing . . . . .Joe Trentacosta, Springer Associates PR

CHINA – THE WHOLE ENCHILADA was originally produced as a Workshop Production of PlayFest! The Harriett Lake Festival of New Plays at the Orlando Shakespeare Theater in Partnership with the University of Central Florida from February 24, 2007 – March 4, 2007. The artists were as follows:

CAST:

PHILIP. . . . . Philip Nolen
ERIC . . . . .Eric Hissom
BRAD. . . . . Brad DePlanche

Director . . . . Jim Helsinger
Stage Manager . . . . .Angi Weiss-Brandt
Assistant Stage Manager . . . . .Joseph Fletcher
Assistant Stage Manager . . . . Katie Rinaldi

CAST

(In order of appearance)

PHILIP
ERIC
BRAD

PLACE

China

TIME

All of it

MUSICAL NUMBERS

ACT 1
1. Disclaimer...All
2. China – The Whole Enchilada...All
3. Peking Man...All
4. Shang...Brad, Philip
5. Chopsticks...Eric, Philip
6. Lotus Shoes...All
7. Khan-Khan...All

ACT 2
1. Evil is a Yellow Face...Philip, Brad
2. Evil is a Yellow Face Reprise...Eric
3. Pie ala Mode...All
4. Stalin...All
5. Is it Wrong?...All
6. Gate of Heavenly Peace...All
7. Enchilada Reprise...All

ACT 1

(The opening bars of Kung Fu Fighting *PLAYS.)*

(lights up)

(GONG)

*(**PHILIP** stands center stage. He wears an elaborate traditional Chinese costume.)*

(A huge map of the world is projected against the back wall.[1] China is highlighted.)

("Made in China" is printed on the map.)

(On stage are five 18"x18" cubes. Each box has a Chinese figure on it.[2])

PHILIP. *(in a bad Chinese accent:)* Ni hao. *(pronounced: "Knee how")*

(He gets the audience to repeat it.)

PHILIP. *(still with the bad accent)* You just learn first Chinese word. Ni hao. Mean "hello." Before we start show, few things. First, turn off cellphone. No cellphone. Cellphone bad. No ring ring ring. Second. No camera. No picture. No click click click. Third. You have candy, unwrap now. No crinkle crinkle crinkle.

*(**ERIC** runs on.)*

ERIC. Philip, Philip! What are you doing?

PHILIP. Ah, Hissom, Eric. Ni hao.

*(**PHILIP** gets the crowd to say "Ni Hao".)*

ERIC. Philip –

---

[1] In the original production, we used rear projections (projections beamed from behind a large screen – not pictures of hind quarters).

[2] In the original production, the figures spelled "to be or not to be." I was torn between that and "don't eat the fried pork."

PHILIP. In China, last name first, first name last. Hissom, Eric. Nolen, Philip.

ERIC. Philip –

PHILIP. Ni hao.

(He gets the audience to say it again.)

ERIC. Philip! What are you doing?

PHILIP. Pre-show announcements.

ERIC. Not the announcements. The accent. We said we weren't doing the accent. We sing about it in the opening number.

PHILIP. *(He drops the accent.)* I know, but I think it works better.

ERIC. It doesn't. It's offensive.

PHILIP. I don't think so.

ERIC. I do. They do.

PHILIP. What's offensive about it?

ERIC. Everything. Everything.

PHILIP. Well if we're going to prepare people to be under China's rule, they better get used to the accent.

ERIC. No accents! No. None. We're not here to make fun of the Chinese.

*(**BRAD** enters dressed in a coolie hat, long braid, huge coke-bottle glasses, buckteeth, an elegant robe and he carries a hookah.[3])*

BRAD. We're not? Dresser!

*(**BRAD** exits.)*

ERIC. We're here to educate people about China. For thousands of years China has been a mysterious country and now that it's becoming a world power –

PHILIP. Dominator, my friend, dominator. It's only a matter of minutes.

ERIC. We want to educate people. Not insult anyone.

---

[3] This is an homage to Mickey Rooney's character, Mr. Yunioshi, in *Breakfast at Tiffany's*. Yes, I know he was a Japanese character but it makes for a terrific politically incorrect first entrance.

PHILIP. Well if my accent is offensive, then I'm a Chinaman.

ERIC. No. No. You see, that's – They're called Chinese.

BRAD. *(from offstage)* Asian-Americans.

ERIC. What?

(**BRAD** *enters.*)

BRAD. They're called Asian-Americans.

ERIC. No they're not.

BRAD. Yes they are.

ERIC. Okay, first off, they're not Americans.

PHILIP. They're Asians.

ERIC. Yes, China is part of Asia –

BRAD. I was told to call them Asian-Americans. It's politically correct, but my mom still calls them Orientals.

PHILIP. So does mine, but she eats at Denny's.[4]

ERIC. They're not rugs.

BRAD. Alright, we'll call them Asian-Americans.

ERIC. They're not Asian-Americans! Look.

(He refers to the map.)

ERIC. Asia is made up of many countries: China, Japan, North Korea, South Korea, Vietnam, Singapore. But there's also India, Pakistan, Afghanistan, Uzbekistan. Do you call someone from Uzbekistan Asian-American?

BRAD. No.

ERIC. Alright. You see.

BRAD. Because you totally made up that name. Uzbekistan. Yeah, right.

ERIC. People see someone with almond shaped eyes and immediately label that person as Asian-American. But it's still offensive because Asia encompasses so much more.

BRAD. You mean you expect me to tell the difference between a guy from South Korea and a guy from North Korea? Fat chance.

---

[4] We also tried: "She's from Alabama." "She voted for George Wallace." "She has Jimmy Swaggart wallpaper." "She has a mullet." "She's voting for Sarah Palin." Feel free to find something current, but Denny's and mullets never go out of style.

PHILIP. That's easy. The North Korean's the one holding the bomb!

BRAD. I'm still going with Asian-American.

ERIC. They're not Americans!

PHILIP. So what are we calling them?

ERIC. Chinese.

BRAD. What are we calling African-Americans?

ERIC. This isn't about African-Americans.

BRAD. You brought it up.

ERIC. I didn't bring –

PHILIP. Yes you did.

ERIC. I…I don't know what we're calling African-Americans.

BRAD. How about African-Americans?

PHILIP. Works for me.

BRAD. Works for me, too.

ERIC. It doesn't work for me.

BRAD. You a racist?

ERIC. No.

BRAD. I think you are.

ERIC. I'm not.

PHILIP. Then what's wrong with African-American?

ERIC. It's presumptuous and jingoistic.

BRAD. Well anyone who's anyone is using the term African-American.

PHILIP. Yeah, it's all the rage. African-American is the new Black.

ERIC. Okay, then what do you call a Black guy from Canada?

PHILIP. Non-existent.[5]

ERIC. No, no. Do you call him African-American or African-Canadian?

BRAD. African-American.

---

[5] At one point I used three punchlines. The other two were: "Phat-Alberta" and "DJ Saskatchafizzle." I ended up cutting them because "non-existent" got such a big laugh. If you're feeling especially politically incorrect, you could use "crime."

ERIC. But he's Canadian.

BRAD. That's not my fault.

ERIC. And you don't see a problem with that?

BRAD. Nope.

ERIC. How about Egypt? Egypt's in Africa. Do you call them African-Americans or Egyptians?

BRAD. That depends.

ERIC. On…?

BRAD. Whether they're African-American or not!

ERIC. You're not – Okay, my uncle was born in South Africa.

BRAD. Your uncle is African-American?

ERIC. Yes.

BRAD. Wow. Who knew?

ERIC. But he's white.

BRAD. An albino African-American?

PHILIP. Freaky, man. Is he all scary looking with red eyes like that hot guy in The DaVinci Code and he had that belt on his leg and he'd pull it and blood would come out of his leg sploosh and it was creepy but kind of sexy –

(Cut him off any time, Eric.[6])

ERIC. No, he's not an albino. He's white. Caucasian.

BRAD. I thought you said he's African-American.

ERIC. Yes.

BRAD. So which is it?

ERIC. Which what?

BRAD. Caucasian or Africa-American?

ERIC. Both. My uncle was born in Africa and he now lives in America. Therefore he's African-American.

PHILIP. Is your sponsor here?[7]

---

[6] Philip could go on for hours at a time if we didn't cut him off. Sometimes Eric wouldn't cut him off and we'd all go out for lunch, come back, and Philip would still be going on and on about how hot the actor was.

[7] Eric's sponsor was never there. He was always at the local bar.

ERIC. We're 'Hyphen-American' happy, but it's presumptuous and jingoistic.

BRAD. Did you just learn those words?

ERIC. Can we just –

BRAD. I think you're a racist.

ERIC. I'm not a racist.

BRAD. Admit it.

ERIC. I'm not a –

BRAD. You're afraid to admit it.

ERIC. I'm not afraid.

BRAD. You're yellow.

ERIC. Would you – Don't use that word.

BRAD. Ah ha! Only a racist would think I meant Asian-Americans.

(**BRAD** *storms off.*)

PHILIP. When China overthrows our country, will we be Asian-Americans or Americasians?

(**PHILIP** *exits.*)

ERIC. Can we just get on with the show?

PHILIP. *(offstage)* Okay.

BRAD. *(offstage)* Racist.

ERIC. I think we're ready to start. So sit back and enjoy China - The Whole Enchilada.

(**ERIC** *exits.*)

(*BLACKOUT*)

(*LIGHTS UP*)

DISCLAIMER SONG

(**ERIC** *enters.*)

ERIC.

CHINA, CHINA MYSTERY
YOUR ANCIENT PAST IS CALLING ME.

(**PHILIP** *enters.*)

PHILIP.

CHINA, CHINA PEARL AND JADE
WHERE EVERYTHING IS INEXPENSIVELY MADE.

(**BRAD** *enters.*)

BRAD.

CHINA, CHINA ALAS
I CANNOT LOCATE YOU ON A WORLD ATLAS.

ALL.

WE ARE HERE TO PROCLAIM
YOUR GLORY AND YOUR FAME
BUT WE REALIZE
WE'RE THREE WHITE GUYS
SO HERE IS OUR DISCLAIM–ER

ERIC.

WE WON'T PRETEND WE'RE CHINESE

PHILIP.

WE WON'T BE WALKING ON OUR KNEES

ERIC & PHILIP.

WE WON'T SWITCH OUR "L'S" AND "R'S"
AND PRETEND THAT WE HAVE SARS

BRAD.

OR SPEAK IN PIG LATIN CANTONESE

ALL.

WE'RE JUST THREE CAUCASIANS
WITH A FASCINATION
WITH THAT NEW SENS-ASIAN
THE CHINESE NATION
YES WE'RE THREE CAUCASIANS
WITH A FASCINATION
WITH THE OVERPOPULATION OF THE CHINESE
NATION

PHILIP.

OUR SHOW IS PRETTY LOWBROW
WAIT TIL YOU SEE ME PLAYING MAO

ERIC.

SO PLEASE DON'T RING OUR NECKS
WHEN I'M ROUND EYE CHIANG KAI-SHEK

BRAD.

    AND THROW US ALL IN THE HOOSEGOW

ALL.

    WE'RE JUST THREE CAUCASIANS
    WITH A FASCINATION
    WITH THAT NEW SENS-ASIAN
    THE CHINESE NATION
    YES WE'RE THREE CAUCASIANS
    WITH A FASCINATION
    WITH THE OVER POPULATION AND THE HUMAN
    RIGHTS VIOLATIONS
    OF THE CHINESE NATION

BRAD.

    WE DON'T WANT TO OFFEND
    WE LIKE TO THINK YOU'RE OUR FRIEND
    BUT IT COULD GET UNRULY
    IF I DRESS UP LIKE A COOLIE

ERIC & PHILIP. You did.

BRAD. Oh, I meant again.

ALL.

    WE'RE JUST THREE CAUCASIANS
    WITH A FASCINATION
    WITH THAT NEW SENS-ASIAN
    THE CHINESE NATION
    YES WE'RE THREE CAUCASIANS
    WITH A FASCINATION
    WITH THE OVER POPULATION AND THE HUMAN
    RIGHTS VIOLATIONS AND THE NUCLEAR ARMS
    PROLIFERATION
    OF THE CHINESE NATION

ALL.

    AND FURTHERMORE WE TELL YOU
    WE WON'T PAINT OUR SKIN PALE YELLOW
    WE WON'T SQUINT OUR EYES LIKE THAT
    OR STIR FRY THE FAMILY CAT

    WE'RE JUST THREE CAUCASIANS
    WITH A FASCINATION
    WITH THAT NEW SENS-ASIAN
    THE CHINESE NATION

YES WE'RE THREE CAUCASIANS
WITH A FASCINATION
WITH THE OVER-POPULATION AND THE HUMAN
RIGHTS VIOLATIONS AND THE NUCLEAR
ARMS PROLIFERATION AND THE WORLDWIDE
DOMINATION AND THE MEGA-CORPORATION AND
THE STUDENT DEMONSTRATIONS AND THE FAMINE
DEVASTATION AND THE HERBAL MEDICATION AND
THE RESTRICTED COPULATION AND THE ONE KID
PROCREATION AND THE SONG ACCELERATION AND
THE UNDER-APPRECIATION
OF THE CHINESE CHINESE NATION
OLE!

ERIC. There. Now no one will be offended. Okay everyone sit back and relax as we take a journey to a magical and mystical land…China.

CHINA - THE WHOLE ENCHILADA

(The boys sit on the cubes and pretend to row.)

ALL.

CHOP CHOP HURRY UP COME ON LET'S GO
THAT OLD SLOW BOAT IS WAY TOO SLOW
THE ORIENT EXPRESS AIN'T FAST ENOUGH FOR ME
'CAUSE WE'VE GOT A LOT TO SEE
FIVE THOUSAND YEARS OF HISTORY
FIVE THOUSAND!? O CRAP WE GOTTA GO!

PHILIP.

THERE'S CHAIRMAN MAO, INFECTED FOWL
WE'LL SHOW YOU HOW YOU SHOULD KOWTOW
THERE'S KUNG PAO, AND EL POLLO GENERAL TSAO

ERIC.

THERE'S KUNG FU, SHIH TZU, PAN-GU, BAMBOO
T'AI CHI, BRUCE LEE, CONGI, YANG-TZE
SHANXI AND BAROQUE CHINOISERIE

BRAD.

THERE'S PEKING, BEIJING, THEY'RE THE SAME THING,
CHONGQING, NANJING, I CHING, LING LING,
DRAGONS HIDING AND SOME TIGERS CROUCHING

ALL.

> THERE'S MAOISM, TAOISM
> COMMUNISM, ERIC HISSOM[8]
> AND WHY THE HELL ARE THEY SO DAMN GOOD AT MATH
> YES IT'S CHINA
> NOT TOSTADA, EMPANADAS, MICHELADA,
> CHIMICHANGA.
> CHINA

PHILIP. Just a small reminder that we're selling Mao piñatas.

ALL.

> YES IT'S CHINA

BRAD. I hope it's not a sign-ah but I think I have angina

PHILIP. This won't play in Carolina 'cause it has a concubina

ERIC. And I think you're gonna finda that our show is asinine-a

ALL.

> YES IT'S CHINA, THE WHOLE ENCHILADA.

> (**PHILIP** exits.)

OVERVIEW

ERIC. China. Cathay. The Celestial Empire. Brad, why don't you give us a quick overview of China.

> (**ERIC** exits.)

BRAD. China, or Asian-America –

> (**ERIC** sticks his head back onstage.)

ERIC. China. It's China. Please call it China.

BRAD. Okay. But if we get complaint letters –

ERIC. Just keep going.

BRAD. China is big. Very big. It's the fourth biggest country in the world.

---

[8] I made Eric change his name to "Hissom" so it would rhyme. I suggest you do the same. If you fail, you can use "Liberalism." It's not nearly as funny but it rhymes.

(He consults the map.)

Only North America, South America, and Everything Else America are bigger. It is the largest country by population: one point three billion people. That means one out of every five people in the world lives in China. So please take a moment to look at the two people on either side of you. If they're not Chinese, you have a long drive home. The Chinese are best known for origami, sumo wrestling, rickshaws, Kabuki Theatre, the attack on Pearl Harbor, sushi, Iron Chef –

*(***ERIC*** sticks his head on stage again.)*

ERIC. Brad, that's Japan! Not China.

BRAD. You just love to stomp all over me.

ERIC. Just skip to the next part.

*(And ***ERIC*** exits.)*

BRAD. Fine. But before we look at the China of today, we must understand the China of yesterday. And I suppose I don't know anything about that either. So let's go back to the beginning. Eric.

BEGINNING

*(***ERIC*** enters as ***BRAD*** starts to exit.)*

ERIC. That's right, Brad. The beginning. The very beginning. The beginningest of beginnings. In the beginning there was nothing but darkness.

(BLACKOUT)

(crash from offstage)

BRAD. Ow.

*(spotlight on ***ERIC***)*

ERIC. The universe –

(crash)

BRAD. Ow.

ERIC. The universe –

(a very long crash)

BRAD. I'm okay.

ERIC. The universe –

  (an extremely long crash)

  *(**ERIC** waits for the "ow.")*

  (nothing)

ERIC. The universe –

BRAD. Ow.

ERIC. The universe is a huge egg floating in a void.

  *(**BRAD** enters and carries a large egg across the stage. He wears a reading headlamp to light the egg.)*

ERIC. The egg hatches and out comes Pan-Gu –

  (A Troll Doll hatches out of the egg.)

BRAD. *(in a high voice)* Mama.

ERIC. – A hairy primordial giant.

BRAD. *(deep voice)* Mama.

ERIC. Pan-Gu pushes the two shells apart. The lower shell becomes the Earth, or Yin, and the upper shell becomes the heavens, or Yang.

  *(**PHILIP** enters dressed as the Pope. He carries a Bible.)*

PHILIP. Really? That's how it happened?

ERIC. Yes.

PHILIP. Pan-Gu.

ERIC. Yes.

PHILIP. Says who?

ERIC. The Chinese.

PHILIP. Really?

ERIC. Yes. Pan-Gu is a Chinese mythological figure –

PHILIP. Mythological indeed.

ERIC. Who created heaven and earth.

PHILIP. Do tell.

ERIC. Pan-Gu grows ten feet a day –

PHILIP. Yeah, right.

ERIC. Pushing the egg shells –

PHILIP. "Heaven" and "Earth."

ERIC. Further and further apart. After eighteen thousand years Pan-Gu bursts apart. His eyes become the sun and moon. His body becomes the mountains, his blood the seas and rivers, his breath the wind, his hair turns into grass and trees, and the fleas that had been living on his skin become the human race.

PHILIP. So the earth is made of Pan-Gu goo?

ERIC. Yes.

PHILIP. That's disgusting.

(**BRAD** *exits.*)

PHILIP. Oh. One question: where did the egg come from?

ERIC. I don't know.

PHILIP. Yeah. Well researched.

(**PHILIP** *exits.*)

PEKING MAN

ERIC. Several billion years pass and then, in northern China, a legend is born.

(**ERIC** *exits.*)

(*MUSIC*)

(**BRAD** *enters, dressed like a prehistoric man.*)

BRAD. (*singing*)
HEY I'M THE PEKING MAN
AND I'LL BE FOUND IN THE PEKING SAND
I KNOW YOU MIGHT BE LEERY
'CAUSE I'M A CHINK IN THE THEORY
OF THAT LAND OF MAKE-BELIEVE
YOU KNOW, THE ONE WITH ADAM AND EVE

IN 1929
I'LL BE AN ARCHEOLOGICAL FIND
THEY'LL FIND MY BONES AND FIRE ASH
I'LL RISE TO FAME WITH GREAT PANACHE
IT'LL BE MY GREATEST THRILL
TO BE THE TALK OF DRAGON BONE HILL

PEOPLE THEY WILL DISCUSS
IF I'M A HOMO ERECTUS
THE NAYSAYERS'LL BE FULL OF CRAP
JUST FEAST YOUR EYES ON THIS PURE SKULLCAP
TELL ME BABY HAVE YOU SEEN
A FINER ONE FROM THE PLEISTOCENE

(spoken)

Good evening, Ladies and Gentlemen and welcome to the Pleistocene Epoch, or what we locals call the Ice Age. Brr. There's a nip in the air and it's not me.

(**PHILIP** *enters.*)

PHILIP. Brad, Brad. Nips are Japs.

BRAD. I thought Nips were Chinese.

PHILIP. No. Nip is short for Nippon. It means Japan in Japanese. Nippon-Nips. Japan-Japs.

(**ERIC** *runs on.*)

ERIC. No! No Nips! No Japs!

BRAD. This is why I like Asian-Americans.

ERIC. They're Chinese.

BRAD. What about Swedes?

ERIC. Swedes?

BRAD. Sweden-Swedes.

ERIC. Swedes is okay.

BRAD. But Nips and Japs are bad.

ERIC. Just sing.

(**ERIC** *and* **PHILIP** *exit.*)

BRAD. *(singing)*
THAT'S RIGHT I'M THE PEKING MAN
AND I'LL BE FOUND IN THE PEKING SAND
IT'LL BE MY CONTRIBUTION
TO THAT THING CALLED EVOLUTION
KANSAS TAKE A LOOK AT ME
'CAUSE I'M A BRANCH OF YOUR FAMILY TREE
I'M THE PEKING…

*(**ERIC** and **PHILIP** enter. **PHILIP** is still dressed as the Pope.)*

ERIC & PHILIP. *(singing)*

HE'S THE PEKING…

BRAD.

I'M THE PEKING…

ERIC & PHILIP.

HE'S THE PEKING…

BRAD.

I'M THE FREAKING PEKING MAN!

ERIC & PHILIP.

HE'S THE PEKING MAN!

BRAD.

LOOK OUT OL' PEKING IS BACK!

ERIC.

LATER THAT DAY GOD SMOTE THE PEKING MAN.

PHILIP.

ALPHA KAZOO!

(Lightning and smiting noise.)

*(**PEKING MAN (BRAD)** dies instantly.)*

PHILIP. Saint Peter sends his regards.

*(**PHILIP** exits.)*

ERIC. Well, that explains the fire ash.

SHANG

*(**BRAD** stacks the boxes to resemble a counter.)*

ERIC. Thousands and thousands of years pass and we find ourselves at the dawn of Ancient China. But that dawn is a little cloudy. You see, scholars aren't really sure when Ancient China began. It's sort of like Camelot or Brigadoon.

BRAD. A Lerner and Loewe musical?

ERIC. No. Mythical.

BRAD. Muthical?

ERIC. Mythical.

BRAD. A mythical muthical?

ERIC. A mythical plathe. A mythical place.

BRAD. Hey your lisp is gone.

ERIC. Go change.

BRAD. Okay.

> (**BRAD** *exits.*)

ERIC. The Shang and Xia Dynasties were things of legend. But in 1899, in a pharmacy outside Beijing, that myth wath thattered. Shattered. That myth was shattered.

> (**ERIC** *exits.*)

> (**BRAD** *and* **PHILIP** *enter.*)

BRAD. So hot. So cold. I need this prescription filled. I have malaria.

PHILIP. Oooo. Malaria. There's a killer.

BRAD. I'm hoping this prescription can cure me.

PHILIP. Yeah, you and a million other dead people.

BRAD. I don't think everyone who's gotten it has –

PHILIP. Think again. It's a deadly killer.

BRAD. That's redundant.

PHILIP. But if this prescription brings you peace of mind while you die a horrible death, then let's get to it. Let's see, deer antler velvet…

> (**PHILIP** *"pours" the ingredients from test tubes into a cup.*)

PHILIP. You know where you got malaria?

BRAD. I don't know, I –

PHILIP. Right here. Good old China. That's right. China, the birthplace of malaria! The Xia Dynasty. Licorice.

> (*He puts licorice in the cup.*)

BRAD. The Xia Dynasty never existed.

PHILIP. Yeah, and you don't have a fever that's about to kill you.

BRAD. Would you please stop saying that.

PHILIP. Licentious goat weed.

(*Goat weed in the cup.*)

BRAD. There's no proof that the Xia or the Shang Dynasty ever existed.

PHILIP. Oh they existed.

BRAD. But there's no proof.

PHILIP. One dragon bone…

(*He starts to put a Magic Eight Ball into the cup.*)

BRAD. Wait. Let me see that.

(**PHILIP** *hands the ball to* **BRAD**.)

BRAD. Oh my Tao!

PHILIP. Hey no swearing in here.

BRAD. This isn't a dragon bone. It's an oracle bone!

PHILIP. Calm down.

BRAD. Calm down!? Oracle bones were used in the Shang Dynasty to divine answers to important questions.

PHILIP. You just said the Shang Dynasty didn't exist.

BRAD. This is proof! This is, this is…

(*Music starts.*)

BRAD.

> IT'S HISTORICAL
> THIS BONE ORACLE
> WE THOUGHT THE SHANG WAS SIMPLY OLD
> FOLKLORICAL
> BUT THIS DRAGON BONE
> THAT YOU ONCE OWNED
> HAS PROVEN THAT THE SHANG ONCE CALLED
> CHINA HOME

PHILIP.

> I'M EUPHORICAL
> THIS BONE ORACLE
> HAS RISEN TO FAME AT SPEEDS METEORICAL
> HOW DOES IT WORK?
> I'LL GO BERSERK
> PLEASE EXPLAIN IT TO THIS PHARMACEUTICAL
> SODA JERK.

BRAD.

> THERE ARE TWO ANSWERS THE YIN AND THE YANG
> YOU THINK OF A QUESTION AS HARD AS YOU CANG
> YOU ROLL THE BONES OF A DEAD BOVINE
> AND THEN YOUR ANSWER WILL BE DIVINED.
>
> *(He thinks as hard as he cang.)*
>
> Is this an actual oracle bone?
>
> *(He shakes the Magic Eight Ball.)*

BRAD. *(reading the Eight Ball)* "It is decidedly so."

PHILIP.

> PHANTASMAGORICAL
> THIS BONE ORACLE
> HAS CREATED A PALPATING JOY IN MY RIGHT
> AURICLE
> MOTHER OF PEARL
> MAY I GIVE IT A WHIRL?
> I'M SO GIDDY AND HAPPY I FEEL LIKE A LITTLE
> SCHOOLGIRL
>
> *(**PHILIP** takes the Eight Ball.)*

PHILIP. Will I get my wontons steamed tonight?

> *(He shakes the Magic Eight Ball.)*

PHILIP. *(reading)* "As I see it, yes."

BRAD & PHILIP.

> IT'S HISTORICAL
> THIS BONE ORACLE
> WE THOUGHT THE SHANG WAS SIMPLY OLD
> FOLKLORICAL
> BUT THIS DRAGON BONE
> THAT YOU ONCE OWNED
> HAS PROVEN THAT THE SHANG ONCE CALLED
> CHINA HOME
> HAS PROVEN THAT THE SHANG ONCE CALLED
> CHINA HOME

PHILIP. Divination!

> *(**PHILIP** hands the cup to **BRAD**.)*

PHILIP. Here you go, pal. It's on the house.

(**BRAD** *drinks the potion and hands the cup back to* **PHILIP**.)

BRAD. Will this potion cure my malaria?

(*He shakes the Ball.*)

BRAD. (*reading*) "Concentrate and ask again." Will this potion cure my malaria?

(*He shakes the Ball.*)

BRAD. (*reading*) "Reply hazy, try again." Will this potion cure my damn malaria?

(*He shakes the Ball.*)

BRAD. (*reading*) "Better not tell you now."

(*He chokes the Magic Eight Ball.*)

BRAD. You stupid piece of crap! The doctor said the prescription would cure me.

(**BRAD** *dies.*[9])

(**PHILIP** *picks up the Magic Eight Ball.*)

PHILIP. (*reading*) "You took out the dragon bone, you idiot."
(*GONG*)

ZHOU

(**PHILIP** *sets up the boxes.*)

PHILIP. Good evening ladies and gentleman and welcome to the Cathay Lounge. We have a change in tonight's program. The Shang Dynasty, which was scheduled to perform, has unexpectedly been replaced by the Zhou Dynasty. So put your eleventh century BC hands together...Eleventh Century BC!?...Talk about an early show. Let's hear it for the Zhou Dynasty.

(**PHILIP** *exits.*)

(**ERIC** *and* **BRAD** *enter. They're a ventriloquist act, dressed in matching outfits, and Brad is the dummy... big surprise.*)

---

[9] We discovered that a Looney Tunes death works best here. Eee, aah, ooo.

ERIC. Good evening. Good evening. Hey, Chester, I have great news.

BRAD. I'm on pins and needles.

ERIC. Yeah, I'm excited, too.

BRAD. No, I'm sitting on pins and needles. What do you have in your pocket?

ERIC. Nothing.

BRAD. I'll be okay. It's just a little prick.

(They look at each other.)

BRAD. Pin prick.

ERIC. Keep it G rated.

BRAD. I'm not the one who's excited.

ERIC. Alright, alright. Can I tell you the good news?

BRAD. Knock yourself out.

ERIC. We just became China's Third Dynasty.

BRAD. Pinch me.

(He does.)

BRAD. Ow!

ERIC. Do you know how we got here?

BRAD. Taxi?

ERIC. The Mandate of Heaven.

BRAD. The what of the who?

ERIC. The Mandate of Heaven. We're here because Heaven didn't like the Shang Ruler anymore.

BRAD. I thought it was because we sacked their capital.

ERIC. That, too. But Heaven said we should be the new act.

BRAD. What do we owe heaven?

ERIC. Ten percent.

(rimshot)

BRAD. We have a drummer?

(wild drumming[10])

---

[10] This was our favorite sound effect and we'd use it randomly to amuse ourselves.

ERIC. Do you know two of the greatest philosophers of all time live during our Dynasty.

BRAD. Do tell.

ERIC. One is Laozi.

BRAD. You just said he's one of the greatest.

ERIC. He is.

BRAD. And now he's lousy?

ERIC. No, his name is Laozi.

BRAD. Okay Mr. My-Name-Is-Better-Than-Yours, what did this Lousy guy do?

ERIC. He's the father of Taoism. He wrote The Tao Te Ching. Tao means "The Way."

BRAD. I wish I knew the way out of here.

ERIC. He said "A journey of a thousand miles starts with a single foot step."

BRAD. Sure, he had legs that worked.

(rimshot)

ERIC. The second philosopher –

(wild drumming[11])

(BRAD *glares at the offstage drummer.)*

ERIC. The second philosopher is Confucius.

BRAD. Him I know.

ERIC. You do?

BRAD. He's a great philosopher.

ERIC. Yes he is.

BRAD. Confucius say, man who drop watch in toilet have crappy time.

ERIC. He didn't say that.

BRAD. Confucius say, man who break wind at church must sit in his own pew.

ERIC. No Confucius didn't –

BRAD. Confucius say, to make egg roll, push it.

---

[11] See what I mean.

ERIC. No, no, you see, those are Confucius Say jokes. Confucius didn't actually say them. They're just jokes.

BRAD. But they start with "Confucius say."

ERIC. I know. But he didn't say them.

BRAD. He should have.

ERIC. Confucius is one of the greatest philosophers to ever live. He teaches kindness. He teaches people to love one another, and to do what is right.

BRAD. Sissy.

*(**ERIC** covers **BRAD**'s mouth then takes his hand away.)*

BRAD. Milksop.

(again with the hand, then off)

BRAD. Moo Goo Gai Pansy.

(They stare at each other.)

ERIC. He says, "Do not do to others what you do not want done to yourself."

BRAD. Thief! He stole that saying from a famous Zhou from Bethlehem.

ERIC. Jesus doesn't arrive for another five hundred years.

BRAD. Hush your mouth.

ERIC. It's true. And Confucius is reduced to juvenile playground puns.

BRAD. You mean, woman who cooks carrots and peas in same pot very unsanitary, isn't a wise saying?

ERIC. No, it's not.

BRAD. I'm not coming to your house for dinner.

ERIC. On the other end of the spectrum is Legalism. Brutal. Tyrannical.

BRAD. Republican.

*(**PHILIP** enters.)*

PHILIP. Okay that's it. Wrap it up. We have a new act coming on.

ERIC. A new act?

PHILIP. Qin the Emperor. And let me tell you, when Qin the Emperor gets here, everyone's gonna jump for joy.

ERIC. He's that good?

PHILIP. You'll not see nothing like the mighty Qin.

> *(rimshot)*
>
> *(gong)*
>
> (**PHILIP** *and* **BRAD** *exit.*)

ERIC. The second half of the Zhou Dynasty is also known as the period of the Warring States. At this time, China, or in Mandarin, Zhouguo, which means Middle Kingdom, is divided into six different states: Han, Wu, Zhou, Chu, Yan, and Qin.

> (**BRAD** *enters. He wears a long robe, a long blonde wig, and elf ears.*)
>
> *("Lord of the Rings"-ish music)*

BRAD. To gain dominion over the Middle Kingdom, a Ring of vast powers is forged by the Dark Lord Sauron in the fires of Mount Doom…Present day Kazakhstan. In the Last Alliance of Elves and the Han, the Ring is cut from Sauron's hand, and is lost in the Yellow River. In 221 BC, the Ring is discovered by Qin Shi Huangdi. The power of the Ring quickly poisons his soul and Qin eats through the other states like a silk worm devouring a mulberry leaf. The Qin Dynasty is born. One Ring now rules them all.

ERIC. Brad, that's mostly Middle Earth and the plot of Lord of the Rings.

BRAD. Thank you for crushing everything I do.

> (**BRAD** *exits.*)

FIRST EMPEROR

ERIC. All hail King Qin.

> (**PHILIP** *enters. He wears a Chinese robe, a cowboy hat and he sounds a lot like President George W. Bush.*)

PHILIP. I don't like King Qin. Sounds too much like "kitchen." I'm changing it to Emperor.

ERIC. All hail Emperor Qin.

PHILIP. I'm like the George Washington of China. The first George Dubya. Let's make it First Emperor.

ERIC. All hail the First Emperor.

PHILIP. And I want you to know I destroyed the other states to unite our country, not divide. I'm a uniter not a divider. My job is to, like, think[12] beyond the immediate. This is historic times. So, mission accomplished.

*(**BRAD** enters.)*

BRAD. First Emperor, I am a scholar and present you with this book I have written of everything that has happened before you.

*(He hands **PHILIP** a book.)*

PHILIP. Nobody needs to know that. Burn all the books. Bury all the scholars alive.

*(**PHILIP** hands the book to **ERIC**, who throws it offstage.)*

BRAD. Did I say 'scholar?" I meant "liar."

PHILIP. I like liars. You can be in my court. Second order of business, somebody find a way for me to live forever.

BRAD. Swallow balls of mercury.

*(**BRAD** hands **PHILIP** a giant box of Whoppers.[13])*

*(**PHILIP** proceeds to "swallow" the Whoppers.)*

PHILIP. You're doing a heck of a job, liar. I like you. I'm not gonna kill you today. Third order of business, just in case these mercury balls don't work, let's start building a tomb for me. Big. I do things in a big way. I want thousands of life size soldiers made to defend me in the after-life. Lots of evil-doers in the after-life. Can't be too careful. What ya gonna make 'em out of?

BRAD. Paper Mache.

PHILIP. Did I say an army of piñatas? Terra-cotta. Terra-cotta's nice. And get about seventy thousand people to build it. But don't tell them they're gonna be buried with me. It ain't good for morale knowing there's no exit strategy.

---

[12] Philip would pause so long here to think about what to say next it could have been considered an intermission. It always made me laugh.

[13] A large box of Sugar Babies was our backup.

ERIC. Yes, Emperor.

PHILIP. Fourthly, we need something to keep unsavory types from coming into our country.

BRAD. How about a huge "Do not enter" sign?

PHILIP. Not all of them can read.

BRAD. How about a dyke?

PHILIP. That's a gay idea.

ERIC. How about a wall?

PHILIP. They can go around it.

ERIC. Not if it's a really long wall.

PHILIP. How long?

ERIC. Over a thousand miles.

PHILIP. That's a long wall. I like it. They'll get tired. What's it gonna be made of?

ERIC. Dirt.

PHILIP. We got somethin' else?

ERIC. No.

PHILIP. Okay. Let's hope it don't rain. Let's build the Long Wall of China.

BRAD. It'll be great.

(**ERIC** *and* **BRAD** *start to exit.*)

PHILIP. But you know, if we really want to keep illegal types out of the country, I have another idea.

(*Uh oh,* **PHILIP** *is going off script.*)

ERIC. Yes, First Emperor?

PHILIP. A fence.

ERIC. *(covering)* A fence? What's a fence?

BRAD. It's like a wall with holes in it.

ERIC. We've never heard of a fence in 220 BC.

PHILIP. A state of the art fence! Fifty feet wide. Coils of barbed wire. Eight feet high. Then a ditch. More barbed wire. A patrol path for vehicles. Closed circuit TVs. Snipers –

ERIC. Ha ha ha. I think the First Emperor is going crazy from all those mercury pills.

PHILIP. It'll keep the Mexicans out.

ERIC. Mongols! It'll keep the Mongols out!

PHILIP. We need a fence dot com. Keep Mexicans in Mexico (*pronounced "Meh-hee-co"*)

ERIC. Mongolia!

PHILIP. Donate today.

> (*sings*)
>
> MY COUNTRY 'TIS OF THEE
> SWEET LAND OF LIBERTY
>
> (*stops singing*)
>
> Hey, these are pretty good.
>
> (*He eats another Whopper and dies.*[14])
>
> (**ERIC** *puts on the cowboy hat.*)

ERIC. After the death of the crazy First Emperor, the legitimate heir is murdered by his younger brother –

> (**BRAD** *kills* **ERIC**.)

BRAD. – who promptly crowns himself Second Emperor.

> (**BRAD** *puts on the cowboy hat.*)

BRAD. To celebrate, the Second Emperor kills his Chief Minister—

> (**ERIC** *becomes the Chief Minister and is killed.*)

BRAD. – and hires a new Chief Minister –

> (**PHILIP** *becomes the new Chief Minister.*)

PHILIP. –who promptly kills the new Second Emperor.

> (**PHILIP** *kills* **BRAD**.)

PHILIP. The new Chief Minister hand-picks a new Third Emperor–um, you—

> (**PHILIP** *places the cowboy hat on* **BRAD**.)

ERIC. And the new Third Emperor wastes no time in killing the new Chief Minister.

> (**BRAD** *kills* **PHILIP**.)

---

[14] Again, Looney Tunes works best. Eee, aah, ooo.

ERIC. It's a tightly contested match, but at the final whistle it's Emperors, three, Chief Ministers, two.

BRAD. And now, a medical warning.

(**BRAD** *exits.*)

ERIC & PHILIP. (*singing to the song* Chopsticks)
THE CHOPSTICK SENSATION
A CHINESE CREATION
TO EAT CHINESE FOOD THEY'RE A MUST
BUT USING THEM TOO LONG
COULD LEAD YOU TO LIFELONG
OSTEOARTHRITIS

(**PHILIP** *and* **ERIC** *exit.*)

(**BRAD** *enters, dressed as Obi-Wan Kenobi.*)

HAN DYNASTY

(*"Star Wars"-ish MUSIC*)

BRAD. In 206 BC, the Han Dynasty, the most important dynasty in Chinese history, is founded by an arrogant smuggler named Han Solo. Han frees a wookie named Chewbacca from enslavement and together the two build the Silk Road, a five thousand mile path made entirely of silk. In Han's absence, Chancellor Palpatine establishes Confucianism as the official doctrine of China. Han Solo returns to China and leads the Rebel strike force against the Imperial forces and Palpatine is killed by the evil Darth Vader.[15]

(**BRAD** *exits as* **ERIC** *enters.*)

WANG MANG

ERIC. The Han Dynasty is briefly interrupted by the Xin Dynasty, founded by Wang Mang, a wily usurper.

(**BRAD** *enters dressed a* **MANG**.)

BRAD. You brought her, you surp her.

ERIC. He's overthrown by China's first secret society, the Red Eyebrows.

---

[15] In the original production, we scrolled Brad's lines on the screen like the opening of Star Wars. Inevitably, we could all see when Brad forgot his lines.

(**PHILIP** *enters. He wears red eyebrows.*[16])

PHILIP. Die, usurper!

(*and kills* **BRAD**)

ERIC. The rebellion throws China into a three-year bloody turmoil.

PHILIP. That's a long period.[17]

ERIC. But a sneaky general tells his troops to paint their eyebrows red as well.

(**ERIC** *slaps on red eyebrows.*)

PHILIP. Red Eyebrow?

ERIC. Yes.

PHILIP. Me, too.

(**ERIC** *kills him and* **PHILIP** *dies all the way offstage.*)

ERIC. Just kidding. And the Red Eyebrows are annihilated.

(**ERIC** *exits.*)

BRAD. Wang Mang is followed by Wang Chung, Connie Chung and Chun King.

(**PHILIP** *enters. He carries a large can of Chung King Chicken Chow Mein.*)

PHILIP. Chun King Chicken Chow Mein, now in the Chun King Divider Pack. Savory sauce and meat in the top can. Crisp bright vegetables in the bottom. Two cans, one neat package. Combine, heat, and serve. It's Cantoneasy.

BRAD. That's right. One taste and you'll be chunking all night.

PHILIP. (*to* **BRAD**) You're not helping.

(**PHILIP** *exits.*)

BRAD. After the fall of the Han Dynasty in A.D. 220, China enters the Age of Division. The political history of the next three and a half centuries is one of the most complex in Chinese history…which is why we're skipping it.

(*He starts to exit.*)

---

[16] Groucho glasses with red tape work like a charm.

[17] This line always scored high on the ol' Groan-O-Meter

BRAD. Oh, Buddhism is introduced to China.

(He exits…)

CARRINGTON DYNASTY

(…and immediately re-enters.)

(Dynasty theme music.)

BRAD. Thank you, Brad. The Carrington Dynasty reaches its peak in season five.

*(**PHILIP** enters.)*

PHILIP. But the Carrington's jump the shark with the Moldavian Massacre, bringing a swift and painful end to the Carrington Dynasty.

(The sound of a needle scratching across a record.[18])

*(**PHILIP** exits.)*

TANG DYNASTY

ERIC. Which brings us to the Tang Dynasty.

*(**BRAD** pulls out a can of Tang.)*

BRAD. The Tang Dynasty, the official Dynasty of the astronauts.

*(**BRAD** exits.)*

LOTUS SHOES

ERIC. The Southern Tang Dynasty, as cool and refreshing as a mint julep on a hot summer's day, gives birth to a cherished and time-honored mother-daughter tradition.

*(**PHILIP** enters, dressed as a woman.)*

PHILIP. Oh Lotus Cup, put down those broken tiles and come here.

*(**BRAD** skips on. He's dressed as a little girl. **BRAD** hops up onto a stack of cubes.)*

PHILIP. Happy birthday, my little lotus cup. You're a big girl now.

---

[18] Record!? Shows you how old I am.

BRAD. *(in a little girl's voice)* Four.

PHILIP. And we must prepare you to get a husband.

BRAD. What's a husband?

PHILIP. I'll explain later.

> *(ERIC hobbles in. He carries a pair of extremely small shoes.)*

PHILIP. Here's your grandmother with your special birthday gift.

ERIC. These were your mother's first shoes. They got her a good man.

BRAD. They're too small, even for me.

PHILIP. We'll make them fit.

BRAD. How?

PHILIP.
> WE'LL BIND YOUR TOES
> BENEATH YOUR FEET
> THAT'S HOW IT'S BEGUN
> AND WHEN YOUR TOES
> BEGIN TO GROW
> THEY'LL SNAP ONE BY ONE
>
> WE'LL BREAK YOUR ARCH
> WITH A LARGE ROCK
> BUT YOU'LL FEEL NO PAIN

ERIC.
> SHE'S LYING DEAR
> IT HURTS SO MUCH
> YOU MAY GO INSANE

ERIC & PHILIP.
> BUT WE'LL WIND YOU
> AND BIND YOU
> IT'S WHAT WOMEN DO
> PLEASE UNDERSTAND
> TO GET A MAN
> YOU MUST WEAR
> LOTUS SHOES
>
> *(ERIC and PHILIP hammer and saw Brad's feet in order to make the shoes fit.)*

BRAD.

> OKAY THAT HURTS
> THAT REALLY HURTS
> I THINK I MIGHT HURL
>
> DEAR FLOWER DRUM
> I DON'T ENJOY
> BEING A GIRL
>
> OH I'M ONLY FOUR
> I'LL RUN NO MORE
> THERE'S SO MUCH TO LOSE
> I DON'T UNDERSTAND
> HOW THIS BEGAN
> I DON'T LIKE
> LOTUS SHOES

PHILIP. *(spoken)* You're not looking at the bright side, dear.

> *(singing)*

> YOUR FOOT WILL BE
> THREE INCHES LONG
> THAT'S ABOUT YEA BIG

BRAD.

> YOU'RE KIDDING ME
> MOM HAVE YOU BEEN
> SWILLING THE SWIG

ERIC.

> YOUR FLESH WILL ROT
> YOUR FEET WILL REEK
> YOU'LL FALL DOWN A LOT
> YOUR HIPS WILL CRACK
> AND THEN YOU WON'T
> BE ABLE TO SQUAT

BRAD.

> OH THE MASOCHIST
> WHO THOUGHT OF THIS
> DID NOT THINK IT THROUGH
> I DON'T UNDERSTAND
> HOW THIS BEGAN
> I DON'T LIKE
> LOTUS SHOES

PHILIP. *(spoken)* I see daylight, Janice.

*(****PHILIP*** *and* ***ERIC*** *hammer and saw some more.* ***BRAD****
opens his mouth to scream but* ***PHILIP*** *puts his hand
over Brad's mouth.)*

PHILIP.
HUSH MY DEAR
DRY YOUR TEARS
IT'S NOT OURS TO CHOOSE
PLEASE UNDERSTAND
TO GET A MAN
ERIC & PHILIP.
WE MUST WEAR
LOTUS SHOES

*(****ERIC*** *and* ***PHILIP*** *exit.)*

*(****ERIC*** *falls and drags himself offstage.)*

BRAD. *(still in the little girl's voice)* For thousands of years
Chinese women have gotten the short end of the
chopstick. China has always been biased to boys for
many reasons: Fear of poverty and neglect, continuity
of lineage, protection in old age, blah blah blah. In
the Book of Songs, an anthology of poems of the Zhou
Dynasty, there's a poem:
"When a son is born, Let him sleep on the bed, Clothe
him with fine clothes, And give him jade to play…
When a daughter is born, Let her sleep on the ground,
Wrap her in common wrappings,

*(****BRAD*** *switches to his own voice.)*

And give broken tiles to play."

Even Confucius said, "One of a woman's virtues lies in
her ignorance."
And China's one-child policy hasn't helped. There are
about seven million abortions in China per year, 70
percent of which are estimated to be of females. And
in the quest to have a son, baby girls have been aban-
doned or "lost."

(He runs his finger across his neck.)

BRAD. Since the one-child policy was initiated in 1979 there have been over fifty million[19] lost daughters of China and it is considered the single biggest holocaust in history.

(**ERIC** *and* **PHILIP** *enter.*)

ERIC. Brad, that's not really funny.

BRAD. No, Eric, it's not.

PHILIP. You used the words "abortion" and "holocaust."

ERIC. This is supposed to be a light-hearted look at China.

BRAD. Yes, I know.

ERIC. That's not really light-hearted.

BRAD. No, I guess it's not.

(**BRAD** *is at a loss for words.*)

BRAD. China also has a one-dog policy.

ERIC. That's better but still not really funny. I mean, now it's gonna be hard to pick up momentum again.

PHILIP. Way to go.

BRAD. I'm sorry.

PHILIP. "I'm sorry" doesn't pick a show up from a screeching halt now does it?

ERIC. Your little speech kidnapped our steam.

PHILIP. Shanghai-ed it, as it were.

ERIC. That's it! Shanghai-ed!

BRAD. *(trying to get the show back on track)* Shanghai's in China, right?

(*They try to get the show rolling again.*)

PHILIP. That's right! That's right! Shanghai's in China!

ERIC. It's the third largest financial city in the world.

PHILIP. And it's the only city in the world whose name means a heinous act.

BRAD. What about Bangkok?

PHILIP. Heinous. With an "H".

---

[19] By 2010 it's estimated to be 80 million.

BRAD. Oh.

(*No one knows what to say or do. Finally they all look at each other…*)

ALL. Chinese fire drill!

(*"Benny Hill"-ish theme song. Played by traditional Chinese instruments is even better.*)

(*They run around. Eventually* **PHILIP** *and* **ERIC** *exit.*)

KHAN-KHAN

BRAD. And then, in 1213, China gets some unexpected visitors.

(**BRAD** *exits.*)

(**ERIC** *enters dressed as Genghis Khan.*)

ERIC.

OH I'M A GREAT MARAUDER
I BROUGHT FEAR AND HORROR
ALL ACROSS CHINA
I WAS A CRAZY MONGOL
BUT WHAT IS REALLY INSANE
I WAS PLAYED BY JOHN WAYNE
IN THE CONQUEROR
I'M GENGHIS KHAN

(**PHILIP** *enters dressed as Kublai Khan.*)

PHILIP.

I AM YOUR SECOND GRANDSON
I'M A LITTLE ROTUND
AND I'M FAMOUS FOR
A BITCHIN' CRIB CALLED XANADU

COLERIDGE WROTE A POEM
HE WAS HIGH ON OPIUM
ABOUT MY PLEASURE-DOME
I'M KUBLAI KHAN

TOGETHER.

OH CAN WE DO THE KHAN-KHAN?

YES WE CAN WE KHAN-KHAN
YES WE CAN WE'RE KHANS
WE'RE GENGHIS KHAN AND KUBLAI KHAN
CAN WE DO THE KHAN-KHAN?
YES WE CAN WE KHAN-KHAN
YES WE CAN WE'RE LIVE
FROM BUDOKAN

WE CAN KHAN-KHAN ALL NIGHT LONG.

YES WE CAN WE LOVE THIS SONG.
BANG A GONG, SING-A-ALONG, IN HONG KONG,
OR ZHEJIANG, PLAY MAH-JONGG, AND PING-PONG,
DRINK OOLONG, EAT DINGDONGS, IN OUR THONGS,
IS THAT IS THAT IS THAT IS THAT IS THAT WRONG?

(**BRAD** *enters dressed as Ricardo Montalban from* The Wrath of Khan.*)*

PHILIP. Ricardo Montalban!?

BRAD. *(sings)*
I LOVE CORINTHIAN LEATHER
I'M A SUAVE JET-SETTER
I WORKED ON A SHOW
WITH A WEE LEPRECHAUN

I CAN ALSO DO THE KHAN-KHAN
YES I CAN I KHAN-KHAN
I WAS IN THE FILM
THE WRATH OF KHAN

ALL.
OH CAN WE DO THE KHAN-KHAN?
YES WE CAN WE KHAN-KHAN
YES WE CAN WE'RE KHANS
WE'RE GENGHIS, KUBE, AND MONTALBAN

PHILIP.
WAIT! WHY WAS MY NAME SHORTENED?
I AM MORE IMPORTANT
THEN OL' MR. ROURKE

BRAD.
THE HELL YOU ARE.

ALL.

WE CAN KHAN-KHAN ALL NIGHT LONG.
YES WE CAN WE LOVE THIS SONG.
BANG A GONG, SING-A-LONG, IN HONG KONG,
OR ZHEJIANG, PLAY MAH-JONGG, AND PING-PONG,
DRINK OOLONG, EAT DINGDONGS, IN OUR THONGS,
IS THAT IS THAT IS THAT IS THAT IS THAT WRONG?

(The Can-Can morphs into a rap song.)

ALL.

CHAKA KHAN! CHAKA KHAN! CHAKA KHAN!

BRAD & PHILIP.

GO GENGHIS! GO GENGHIS! IT'S YOUR BIRTHDAY!
IT'S YOUR BIRTHDAY!

ERIC.

BACK IN THE DAY I HAD SOME MIGHTY FORCES
WE STORMED DOWN ON TINY LITTLE HORSES
IF I STAYED AROUND I WOULDA TAKEN EUROPE
I'LL LET YOU IN, THE SECRET'S IN THE STIRRUPS
THE GREAT WALL I THINK IT'S ONLY –

BRAD & PHILIP.

SO SO!

ERIC.

WHEN I JUMPED OVER EVERYONE SAID –

BRAD & PHILIP.

OH NO!

PHILIP.

HISTORY SAYS YOU'RE SOME KIND OF VILLAIN

ERIC.

I'M A MEAN MOTHER MONGOL BENT ON COSA
NOSTRA KILLIN'

BRAD & PHILIP.

HE'S OLD SCHOOL G!

ERIC.

I'M OLD SCHOOL G!

BRAD & PHILIP.

HE'S OLD SCHOOL G!

ERIC.

I'M OLD SCHOOL G!

BRAD & PHILIP.

HE'S OLD SCHOOL G!

PHILIP.

MY EMPIRE WAS THE LARGEST IN HISTORY
STRETCHING FROM IRAQ TO THE SHORE OF THE
CHINA SEA
I DIDN'T LIKE THE HAN, THEY DIDN'T LIKE ME
SO I TAXED THEM AND LET MY PEEPS GO TAX-FREE
I GOT A HOMEBOY HE COMES FROM ITALY
HE CALLS ME CAPO DI TUTTI CAPI[20]
WE RULE BUT WE DO NOT SLAUGHTER
HE'S MARCO –

BRAD & ERIC.

POLO!

PHILIP.

MARCO –

BRAD & ERIC.

POLO!

PHILIP.

MARCO –

BRAD & ERIC.

POLO!

PHILIP.

MARCO –

BRAD & ERIC.

POLO!

PHILIP.

FISH OUTTA WATER!

ERIC & PHILIP.

WE STARTED THE YUAN DYNASTY.
Y TO THE U TO THE A TO THE ENEMY.
WE STARTED THE YUAN DYNASTY.
Y TO THE U TO THE A TO THE ENEMY.
WE STARTED WE STARTED WE STARTED WE STARTED
WE STARTED WE STARTED

(Music stops.)

---

[20] It's Italian for the "Boss of all bosses." And did you know that the line "I'm going to make him an offer he can't refuse" from *The Godfather* ranks #2 on the AFI Famous Movie Quotes?

BRAD. Let's end this little French ditty.

(Music starts up.)

ALL.

OH CAN WE DO THE KHAN-KHAN?
YES WE CAN WE KHAN-KHAN
YES WE CAN WE KHAN
WE'RE GENGHIS, KUBE, AND MONTALBAN
WE CAN DO THE KHAN-KHAN
YES WE CAN WE KHAN-KHAN
YES WE CAN WE'RE KHANS
NOT MADELINE KHAN
BUT GENGHIS KHAN
NOT SAMMY CAHN
BUT KUBLAI KHAN
NOT JIMMY CAAN
BUT MONTALBAN
WE'RE KHANS, WE'RE KHANS, WE'RE KHANS, WE'RE KHANS
WE'RE KHANS, WE'RE KHANS, WE'RE KHANS, WE'RE KHANS
WE'RE KHANS, WE'RE KHANS.

(They finish by striking William Shatner's infamous pose from "The Wrath of Khan", *arms raised to the sky.)*

ALL.

KHAN!!!

(BLACKOUT)

End Act 1

ACT 2

(Lights up. The boys are on stage.)

PHILIP. When we last left China, the Mongol Nation sang and danced its way to victory over the Chinese.

BRAD & ERIC. Khan!

PHILIP. But during intermission the Chinese decide they're weary of Mongol rule and their little Mongol reign of terror.

BRAD & ERIC. Grumble grumble grumble.

PHILIP. And decide to overthrow the Mongols.

BRAD & ERIC. Topple topple topple.

PHILIP. But the Mongols have banned group gatherings so it's impossible to make a plan. Spread out!

BRAD & ERIC. Foiled foiled foiled.

PHILIP. But one Chinese rebel gets an idea.

BRAD. I have an idea. The Moonpie Festival!

ERIC. The Mooncake Festival.

BRAD. Have you ever had a mooncake? They're disgusting. Moonpies are much better.[21]

ERIC. Moonpies have nothing to do with the Mooncake Fest –

BRAD. Okay. Ding-Dongs. We'll go with Ding-Dongs. Happy now?

*(**ERIC** exits.)*

BRAD. *(starting the scene again)* I have an idea. The Ding-Dong Festival, when we Chinese like to eat Ding-Dongs. We'll slip a piece of paper with revolution information on it in each Ding-Dong we hand out for the Festival. But instead of eating the Ding-Dongs, we'll overthrow the Yuan Dynasty.

*(**BRAD** walks up to **PHILIP**.)*

BRAD. Ding-Dong?

PHILIP. Who's there?

*(**BRAD** hands **PHILIP** an imaginary Ding-Dong.)*

*(**PHILIP** reads the message inside.)*

---

[21] It's true.

PHILIP. *(reading)* Say hello to my little friend![22]

(**BRAD** *kills* **PHILIP**.)

PHILIP. Ow. Son of a –

(**PHILIP** *exits.*)

(**ERIC** *enters.*)

ERIC. And on the fifteenth day of the eighth moon in the year 1368, the Yuan Dynasty is overthrown and the Ming Dynasty now rules China.

BRAD. All thanks to the Ding-Dong.

ERIC. Mooncake. All thanks to the mooncake.

BRAD. A piece of paper with a message on it inside a Ding-Dong becomes an instant sensation but the creamy filling proves too messy. However, in 1369 China celebrates the birth of the fortune cookie.[23]

ERIC. In 1371, after the Emperor reads aloud his fortune "You will be unfortunate in all things" a court eunuch adds…

BRAD. "In bed."

ERIC. The tradition sticks. The eunuch is killed.

(**ERIC** *kills* **BRAD**.)

(**ERIC** *exits.*)

MING

BRAD. Later in 1371, the Emperor and founder of the Ming Dynasty, the evil Emperor Ming the Merciless, moves the capital of China from Beijing to the planet Mongo.

(**BRAD** *exits.*)

(**PHILIP** *enters, dressed as Ming the Merciless from the Flash Gordon comic strip.*)

PHILIP. I am Ming the Merciless, Emperor of the planet Mongo. I am evil, yellow, and definitely Chinese. Soon I will rule the entire universe and no one can stop me.

(Flash Gordon MUSIC)

---

[22] This is the famous quote from *Scarface*. It ranks #61 on the AFI Famous Movie Quotes, narrowly beating out "What a dump," which may be more appropriate for this play.

[23] A lie. A complete and utter lie.

(**BRAD** *enters as Flash Gordon.*)

BRAD. No one but Flash Gordon, world-renowned polo player and Yale graduate.

(**ERIC** *enters.*)

ERIC. What are you guys doing!?

PHILIP. The beauty of the female pleases me.

(**ERIC** *looks around. What female?*)

(**PHILIP** *slaps a wig on him.*)

PHILIP. She shall be my wife. The young man shall be slain.

(**BRAD** *rushes up to* **ERIC** *and hugs him.*)

BRAD. These arms were meant to hold and protect you and, by heaven they will, as long as they have life.

PHILIP. Send him to the firing squad.

BRAD. Oh well, it's been nice knowing you.

(*Zap! Zap!* **PHILIP**'s *invisible powers force* **BRAD** *off-stage.*)

(*A couple of gunshots are fired offstage.*)

BRAD. (*offstage*) Ha. You missed. I can't believe every one of you –

(*More shots are fired.*)

BRAD. (*from offstage*) Okay. One or two of you got me that –

(*A machine gun fires off a zillion shots.*)

BRAD. (*offstage*) Yeah, you all got me that time.

PHILIP. Dale Arden, as you know, we on this planet have progressed far beyond you earthlings. And when I say "we" I mean the Chinese. And when I say "earthlings" I mean Westerners. The reason for our success is that we possess none of the human traits of kindness, mercy, or pity. We are coldly scientific and ruthless. You are to be one of us. And when I say "us" I mean the Chinese.

ERIC. What!?

PHILIP. Bring out the Dehumanizing machine.

(**BRAD** *enters as Fu Manchu.*)

BRAD. Not so fast, Ming.

PHILIP. Fu Manchu! Do you have the Dehumanizing Machine?

BRAD. It's no use, Ming.

PHILIP. The dehumanizing machine is broken?[24] Again? I knew I should have gotten the extended warranty. But it was two hundred dollars and I felt he was just up-selling me, and the manufacturer's warranty was good for two years. I never know if I should –

BRAD. Let her go.

PHILIP. What!?

BRAD. We'll never rule the universe.

PHILIP. Have you been playing with the dehumanizing machine?

BRAD. Our Yellow Empire is an opium pipe dream.

PHILIP. What!?

BRAD. World domination doesn't work. It didn't work for Hitler or Stalin or –

PHILIP. Amateurs!

(music)

PHILIP. They didn't possess the secret to world domination: the cruel cunning of an entire Eastern race.

Song - *"EVIL IS A YELLOW FACE"*

PHILIP.

> BEFORE THE NAZIS
> AND THOSE PINKO COMMIES
> WE WERE THE ONES THE WORLD LOVED TO FEAR
> KINGS OF PULP FICTION
> WE RULED WITH BAD DICTION
> I LOVED EVERY BOO, HISS AND SCURRILOUS JEER
> EVIL WAS A YELLOW FACE
>
> BUT I WATCHED IN DISGRACE
> AS WE DROPPED TO THIRD PLACE
> THE NAZIS AND RUSKIES ROSE TO THE TOP
> AND NOW THERE'S AL-QAEDA
> WITH THEIR JIHADS AND FATWAS
> I'M TELLING YOU FU THIS HAS GOT TO STOP
> WE'RE NO ORDINARY MALCONTENTS

---

[24] The quality of dehumanizing machines has really gone downhill in recent years. It's nearly impossible to get a good one.

WE'RE ARCH VILLAINS FROM THE ORIENT
WE'RE MING AND FU MANCHU
THE DREADED SLANT EYED TWO
OUT TO DESTROY THE HUMAN RACE
EVIL IS A YELLOW FACE

(**PHILIP** *laughs an evil laugh.*)

(**PHILIP** *and* **BRAD** *are too caught up in the song so* **ERIC** *easily escapes.*)

BRAD.

MING YOU ARE SO RIGHT
LET OUR KINGDOMS UNITE
OUR BLOOD MIX TOGETHER AND COAGULATE

IT'S TIME TO ROAR BACK
WITH A WORLDWIDE ATTACK
THAT WILL SCARE WHITEY SO A BRICK HE'LL
DEFECATE

BRAD & PHILIP.

WE'RE NO ORDINARY MALCONTENTS [25]
WE'RE ARCH VILLAINS FROM THE ORIENT

PHILIP.

WE'RE MING

BRAD.

AND FU MANCHU

BRAD & PHILIP.

THE DREADED SLANT EYED TWO
OUT TO DESTROY THE HUMAN RACE
EVIL IS A YELLOW FACE

(**ERIC** *exits.*)

(**PHILIP** *and* **BRAD** *laugh evil laughs, which turns into coughing.*)

PHILIP.

OOO, A LITTLE VOMIT.

BRAD & PHILIP.

WE'RE TWO EVIL CARCINOGENS
WE'RE SO EVIL WE'RE PLAYED BY WHITE MEN

---

[25] In the original production, Eric entered by doing a cartwheel. He was dressed like a Bond girl and danced during the chorus. And boy, was he hot.

PHILIP.

BORIS KARLOFF.

BRAD.

BRITISH.

PHILIP.

WARNER OLAND.

BRAD.

SWEDISH.

PHILIP.

CHRISTOPHER LEE.

BRAD.

BRITISH.

PHILIP.

MAX VON SYDOW.

BRAD.

SWEDISH.

BRAD & PHILIP.

WHAT IS IT WITH THE SWEDES AND BRITS?
AND WHY CAN'T WE SAY JAPS AND NIPS?

BRAD. I mean really, why can't we? You listen to 50 Cent and every other word is either bitch or ni –

PHILIP.

SO HERE IS OUR WARNING
A NEW DAY IS DAWNING
THE NIGHTMARE YOU FEARED HAS NOW FIN'LLY
AWOKE

BRAD.

WE'LL BREED WITH YOUR WOMEN
KILL YOU WHILE WE'RE GRINNIN'
BECAUSE WE HAVE ALSO

BRAD & PHILIP.

PEED IN YOUR COKE
WE'RE NO ORDINARY MALCONTENTS [26]
WE'RE ARCH VILLAINS FROM THE ORIENT

PHILIP.

WE'RE MING

---

[26] Eric then entered, walking on his hands. He made it to centerstage, fell over, hurt his shoulder, and limped off. Nothing like upstaging two evil arch villains.

BRAD.
　AND FU MANCHU

BRAD & PHILIP.
　THE DREADED SLANT EYED TWO
　OUT TO DESTROY THE HUMAN

PHILIP.
　AND WHEN I SAY "HUMAN" I MEAN

PHILIP & BRAD.
　THE WRETCHED WHITE MAN'S RACE

BRAD & PHILIP.
　EVIL IS A YELLOW FAAAAAAAAAAA –

PHILIP. *(spoken)* Take it up the octave.

BRAD & PHILIP.
　——AAAAAAAAAAAAAAAACE![27]

PHILIP. And now, Dale Arden –

　(He looks but **ERIC** *is gone.)*

PHILIP. Dale Arden –? How can we create an evil Yellow empire if we don't have white women to breed with?

　*(***BRAD*** *looks out into the audience.)*

BRAD. Well there are plenty of white women out there.

　*(***ERIC*** *enters dressed as Charlie Chan.)*

ERIC. Stop right there!

PHILIP. Dale Arden–!

BRAD. Wow! Dale Arden, you are closing time ugly. It's like make-up on a pig. Are there any other white women?[28]

ERIC. I'm not Dale Arden, you idiots! There's a new yellow face in town. Charlie Chan.

---

[27] Philip usually threw in an adlib at the end of the song. Something like "That's worth $15" or "You don't get that at Equus."

[28] In rehearsal, I gave Brad a list of insults to choose from. When we ran the scene he read the entire list and we all collapsed from laughter. Here's the original list: "Honey, you're a two-bagger." "Woof." "You are closing time ugly." "Wow, you are ugly." "It's like make-up on a pig." "Did your neck just throw up?" "Your face looks like my armpit." "Are your parents cousins?" "My milk just turned into yogurt." "Someone's been playing with the ugly stick." "Are there any other white women?"

PHILIP. Chan! You're no match for two evil arch villains. Didn't you listen to our song?

ERIC. You forget. I, too, was played by Warner Oland.

PHILIP. Okay, seriously, what is it with the Swedes?

ERIC. And that's not Fu Manchu!

(What!?)

ERIC. That's –

*(**ERIC** removes Brad's hat and slaps dog ears on him.)*

ERIC. Hong Kong Phooey.

BRAD. Number one super guy.

ERIC. Two against one. We win.

(The following dialogue is rapid fire and overlapping.)

PHILIP. No, we have two. We win. Ming and Fu Manchu.

ERIC. I'm Charlie Chan. He's Hong Kong Phooey.

PHILIP. But he was Fu Manchu first.

ERIC. He changed his mind.

PHILIP. He didn't change his mind. You put dog ears on him.

ERIC. Two against one. We win.

PHILIP. You don't win.

ERIC. We're two. You're one.

PHILIP. Oh yeah!? Well I'm an arch villain. That's like three regular villains.

ERIC. You're not three villains.

PHILIP. I win three to two.

ERIC. You don't win three to two.

PHILIP. Villains count as one. But arch villains are way more than one.

ERIC. Arch villains count as one villain. One.

PHILIP. Maybe even four or ten villains.

ERIC. Ten? You're one villain.

PHILIP. No. Arch villains aren't normal. I'd be just a villain.

ERIC. How many of you do I see? One.

PHILIP. But I'm an *arch* villain.

ERIC. How many of us do you see? Two. Two is more than one. We're moving on.

PHILIP. We're not moving on.

ERIC. We're two. You're one. You lost.

PHILIP. You cheated.

ERIC. I didn't cheat.

PHILIP. Did, too.

ERIC. Did not.

PHILIP. I have an evil Yellow Empire.

ERIC. Your empire crumbled.

PHILIP. We're like taxi cabs in New York City.

ERIC. Cabs? Cabs? What are you talking about?

PHILIP. We're everywhere. Taking over the world. I have an evil Yellow empire.

ERIC. You lost. We're moving on.

PHILIP. Put the hat back on.

*(**PHILIP** puts Brad's hat back on him.)*

ERIC. He's not putting the hat back on.

*(**ERIC** pulls the hat off and hands **BRAD** the ears.)*

ERIC. Put the ears on.

*(**BRAD** puts the ears on.)*

PHILIP. Put the hat back on.

(The ears come off and the hat goes on.)

ERIC. No the hat doesn't go on. Put the ears back on.

(Hat off. Ears on.)

PHILIP. Hat.

(Ears off. Hat on.)

PHILIP. Look he's Fu Manchu. I win.

(Hat off. Ears on.)

ERIC. He's Hong Kong Phooey. I win.

PHILIP. I win. I win. I win.

ERIC. I win. I win. I win.

BRAD. Hong Kong Phooey Chop!

    (**BRAD** *karate chops* **PHILIP**.)

PHILIP. Ow! What the–?

ERIC. I win!!!

    (**ERIC** *and* **BRAD** *win!* **PHILIP** *storms off.*)

PHILIP. This isn't over, Chan!

    (*And exits.*)

BRAD. Have you seen my Hong Kong Book of Kung Fu?

ERIC. Just get ready for the next part.

    (**BRAD** *sets up for the next part.*)

    (*MUSIC*)

    REPRISE

ERIC.

    SAX ROHMER WROTE FU MANCHU
    DID YOU KNOW HE DIED OF ASIAN FLU
    THE GUY WHO CREATED FLASH
    DIED IN A FREAK CAR CRASH
    IF THEY ONLY KNEW
    INSTANT KARMA WILL GET YOU

    (**ERIC** *exits.*)

INVENTIONS

BRAD. Some of the greatest inventions in the world come from China. Here to demonstrate those inventions are two of the most famous inventors of all time—

PHILIP. *(from offstage)* American inventors!

BRAD. American inventors: Ben Franklin and Thomas Edison.

    (**ERIC** *enters dressed as Ben Franklin.*)

    (**PHILIP** *enters dressed as Thomas Edison. He's still pissed off.*)

ERIC. Good evening. You know, Tom, looking out at this crowd I'm reminded of the time I said, "Fish and visitors stink after three days."

PHILIP. So does that joke.

ERIC. Okay. You know, Thomas Edison, you and I have something in common.

PHILIP. We both tagged Phyllis Diller?

(**ERIC** *shoots him a look.* **PHILIP** *has gone off the deep end.*)

PHILIP. We both dorked Phyllis Diller?

(*Philip!!*)

PHILIP. Phyllis Diller?

ERIC. Electricity! I discovered electricity and you invented the electric light bulb.

PHILIP. Actually I didn't invent the electric light bulb. A lot of people before me are credited with inventing it. Sir Humphrey Davy, Joseph Swan, Nikola Tesla. I let them do the hard work and then I mass produced it.

(**ERIC** *looks at him. "What the hell are you doing?")*

ERIC. Well, if it wasn't for the Chinese, I never would have discovered electricity and you never would have invented the electric light bulb.

PHILIP. I said I didn't invent the –

ERIC. I know! Ha ha ha. Did you know the Chinese invented this?

(**ERIC** *holds up a kite.*)

PHILIP. Yes.

(*That wasn't the right answer.*)

ERIC. Well…Not everyone knows that the Chinese invented the kite.

PHILIP. Maybe the Chinese should all go fly their kites instead of taking over the world.

ERIC. Oh ho ho, Tom, you and your odd, politically incorrect sense of humor.

PHILIP. I'm just the messenger.

ERIC. Deliver it somewhere else. Moving right along…

(**ERIC** *looks at* **PHILIP**. *Obviously it's Philip's line but* **PHILIP** *is stewing.*)

ERIC. Perhaps there's an invention you'd like to demonstrate.

(**ERIC** *nudges a china bowl towards* **PHILIP**.)

ERIC. Something about *china*.

(**PHILIP** *continues to sulk. And then* –)

PHILIP. I won three to two.

ERIC. You didn't win three to two.

PHILIP. I was an evil arch villain.

ERIC. Would you let it go! Ha ha. Perhaps there's an invention –

PHILIP. Oh yes. An ingenious invention.

(**PHILIP** *pulls out a bottle of water and pours it into the bowl.*)

PHILIP. First I fill this bowl with a little water.

ERIC. Yes. Into the china bowl.

(**PHILIP** *pulls out a turkey baster. A turkey baster!?*)

PHILIP. And then I take this turkey baster –

(*He proceeds to fill the baster with water.*)

PHILIP. And fill it with water.

(**PHILIP** *is really going off script.*)

ERIC. From the china bowl.

PHILIP. I need a volunteer.

(*He pinches Eric's butt.*)

ERIC. Ow!

PHILIP. Thank you, Ben.

ERIC. I didn't –

PHILIP. And I take the baster –

(*He places it a few inches above Eric's head and slowly drops water on his head, a drop at a time.*)

ERIC. Oh look, this bowl of water is very interesting. It's china. I didn't notice that before. Well I'll be. The Chinese invented China. Porcelain China. Fine China.

PHILIP. You don't find that odd?

ERIC. No.

PHILIP. Everybody has fine china. Good china. No one has bad china.

(The water is driving **ERIC** *crazy.)*

ERIC. Why would you want bad china?

PHILIP. Exactly. Good china. We all want good china. Good china. It's almost hypnotic. Good china. Good china.

*(***ERIC** *struggles to go on.)*

(He picks up some long needles.)

ERIC. The healing powers of acupuncture were first discovered in China.

PHILIP. That's a great invention.

ERIC. Yes, it's very restorative.

PHILIP. Needles jabbed into your body. That's great. I think they also invented the hot poker in the eye.

*(***PHILIP** *shoots water in Eric's eye.)*

ERIC. Stop it! That's driving me nuts!

PHILIP. It's suppose to. Chinese water torture.

ERIC. The Chinese did not invent Chinese water torture.

PHILIP. Then why is it called Chinese water torture?

ERIC. I happen to know the answer. One of Harry Houdini's escapes was called the Chinese Water Torture Cell and ever since then people have associated water torture with the Chinese.

PHILIP. Yeah, sure, blame Houdini, aka Ehrich Weiss. It's always the Jews with you, isn't it, Franklin?

*(***ERIC** *picks up two pieces of paper.)*

ERIC. I hold here the Constitution of the United States and our Declaration of Independence, the foundations of our country and written on yet another Chinese invention. Paper.

*(***PHILIP** *grabs the paper.)*

PHILIP. And the Chinese also invented the paper cut.

*(***PHILIP** *slices Eric's hand with the paper.)*

ERIC. Ow. Son of a –! Ow! Ow! Oh! Ow, that hurts like a –!

PHILIP. No bleeding. Invisible to the naked eye. But unimaginable pain. Skillful and cunning. Maybe if they impaled you with an acupuncture needle it would feel better.

(And **PHILIP** *does just that.)*

ERIC. Ow! What the –!?

PHILIP. And if I'm not mistaken, Sun Tzu's The Art of War is also written on paper. Here's your Declaration of Independence. You can use the other side to write our Declaration of Surrender.

(He hands it to **ERIC.** *)*

(Another paper cut.)

ERIC. Ow!

*(***ERIC*** grabs a handful of spaghetti.)*

ERIC. Spaghetti! Ow!

PHILIP. Oops. Lemon butter sauce. You need another acupuncture needle.

*(***PHILIP*** sticks him again.)*

ERIC. Ow! The Chinese invented spaghetti. Yum yum.

PHILIP. Yes. So we can overload on carbohydrates, making us fat, sluggish, and easily conquered.

ERIC. The abacus –

(He holds up an abacus.)

PHILIP. Which they'll use to calculate how much gold they've plundered at Fort Knox.

*(***ERIC*** holds up a compass.)*

ERIC. The compass –

PHILIP. And gunpowder, cannons, bombs –

ERIC. Stop it, Philip! Right now! Just stop it!

PHILIP. What?

*(***ERIC*** and **PHILIP** rip off their costumes and set up for the next part.)*

ERIC. What what!? What are you doing!? China has made extraordinary achievements to mankind and you're out here making them seem like a bunch of war mongers.

PHILIP. Well if the fu shits.

ERIC. If the shoe fits!

PHILIP. So you agree.

ERIC. No! The shoe does not fit! And I don't even want to talk about your Ming the Merciless act.

PHILIP. Brad was Fu Manchu.

ERIC. Brad's an idiot!

BRAD. *(from offstage)* I have feelings.

ERIC. You are single-handedly reviving Yellow Peril.

*(**BRAD** enters. He carries a yellow pillow.)*

BRAD. Yellow Pillow!

ERIC & PHILIP. Yellow Peril!

BRAD. Oh.

(He exits.)

ERIC & PHILIP. Idiot.

YELLOW PERIL

ERIC. It all started in the United States in 1840.

*(**ERIC** exits.)*

PHILIP. Welcome to the United States 1840. What can I do for ya?

BRAD. I'd like to come in.

PHILIP. You and every other foreigner.

BRAD. America. Land of hopes. Land of dreams. Land o' lakes.

PHILIP. You trying to butter me up? Where ya from?

BRAD. China.

PHILIP. What's the password?

BRAD. Swordfish?

PHILIP. Good guess but that was yesterday's password. Guess again.

BRAD. Freedom?

PHILIP. We have a winner. Come on in. And congratulations, you're our first Chinaman.

(*But before* **BRAD** *can pass into the Land of Milk and Honey,* **ERIC** *enters dressed as an Italian.*)

ERIC. There's a gold in a them hills!

(**PHILIP** *lets* **ERIC** *pass by.*)

PHILIP. Benvenuto.

ERIC. Grazie.

PHILIP. Prego.

(**BRAD** *starts to walk passed* **PHILIP**.)

(**PHILIP** *stops him.*)

PHILIP. Hey where are you going?

BRAD. You just let me in.

PHILIP. No I didn't.

BRAD. You said welcome to the United States 1840.

PHILIP. We changed the policy.

(**PHILIP** *dings a small bell.*)

PHILIP. It's now the United States 1848.

BRAD. That was fast.

PHILIP. What's the password?

BRAD. Freedom.

PHILIP. I'm sorry. That was yesterday's password.

(**ERIC** *walks up dressed as an Irishman.*)

PHILIP. Can I help you?

ERIC. (*Irish accent*) Somebody ate all me frosted lucky charms.

PHILIP. That's tough potatoes, mic. Hey look at the two of you. Rice and Potatoes. That's too much starch.
(*to* **BRAD**)
I said "light starch!"
(*to* **ERIC**)
What's the password?

ERIC. Cheap gold mine labor.

PHILIP. Come on in.

    (**ERIC** *walks passed* **PHILIP.**)

    (**BRAD** *walks up to* **PHILIP.**)

BRAD. Cheap gold mine labor.

ERIC. 1850.

    (*ding*)

PHILIP. Policy change.

    (*to* **BRAD**)

You have to pay a Foreign Miners Tax.

BRAD. But I'm over eighteen.

PHILIP. Not that kind of minor. Asia Miners.

    (**BRAD** *pays him.*)

BRAD. Now can I come in?

PHILIP. Sure, come on in –

ERIC. 1854.

    (*ding*)

PHILIP. Policy change. You can come in but you can't testify against the white man in court.

BRAD. I don't know any white men. I just want to work and send my kids to school.

ERIC. 1859.

    (*ding*)

PHILIP. Policy change.

BRAD. What now?

PHILIP. You can't send your kids to school in San Francisco.

BRAD. But that's where we're going to live.

PHILIP. Not anymore. It's too bad, too. San Francisco has a great Chinatown, if you like Chinatown. Frankly I didn't. I preferred Bonnie and Clyde but they've *Dunaway* with those kind of films. [29]

    (*pause for either groans or silence*)

---

[29] There will most likely be groans if it's an older audience. If it's a younger audience, there will most likely be deafening silence.

PHILIP. I said they've Dunaway with those kind of films.

(Anyone? Anyone?)

There was a time you could Faye Dunaway and get a laugh. But you had to fay it with a lifp. Faye Dunaway fans? Anyone?

*(He turns backs to **BRAD**.)*

PHILIP. Come on in, China. You can build our railroads.

*(to **ERIC**)*

Hey Irish. Good news. You're no longer the scum of America.

ERIC. 1870.

(ding)

*(**PHILIP** stops **BRAD** from entering.)*

PHILIP. I'm sorry. Policy change. Are you African?

BRAD. No, I'm Chinese.

PHILIP. That's too bad. Africans just got the right to become citizens, but not you Chinese.

BRAD. That's okay. We just want to get into America. My wife and I will figure –

PHILIP. A wife!? What kind of a place do you think this is? You can't bring your wife in here.

BRAD. I can't?

PHILIP. She has to go back to Chinaland.

BRAD. But she's my wife.

PHILIP. Someone should have spoken up at the wedding.

ERIC. 1882.

(ding)

PHILIP. Policy change.

BRAD. What do you want now?

PHILIP. We want you to go back to Chinaland with your wife.

BRAD. But you were about to let me in.

PHILIP. We changed our minds. No Chinese for us. We superior whites have to exclude you inferior Asiatics, by law, or, if necessary, by force of arms. But congratulations. You Chinese are the first people in United

States history to be officially named undesirable for immigration. Ha. You're not even wretched refuse. [30] Come back in ten years.

ERIC. 1892.

(ding)

PHILIP. Policy change.

BRAD. I'm back.

PHILIP. Ten years already?

BRAD. Time flies like an arrow.

PHILIP. Fruit flies like a banana.

BRAD. I'd like to come in.

PHILIP. And we'd like you to go back to Chinaland. You're taking away all of our jobs. Come back in another ten years.

ERIC. 1902.

(ding)

PHILIP. Policy change.

BRAD. I'm back.

PHILIP. You're like a bad penny.

BRAD. That doesn't make sense.

PHILIP. Of course not. It's singular. If it was plural it would make cents.

BRAD. Can I come in now?

PHILIP. No.

BRAD. I'll see you in ten years.

PHILIP. That's what you think. We're never letting you in.

BRAD. Never!?

PHILIP. You're a threat to western civilization. We won't be part of your evil Yellow Empire.

ERIC. 1943.

(ding)

---

[30] It's a reference to "The New Colossus," the poem at the base of the Statue of Liberty: "Give me your tired, your poor, Your huddled masses yearning to breathe free, The wretched refuse of your teeming shore. Send these, the homeless, tempest-tossed, to me: I lift my lamp beside the golden door."

PHILIP. *(overly friendly and loving)* Policy change. Hey where have you been? So good to see you. We're allies. We're both fighting the Japs. Oh we've locked up a bunch of 'em here. Let's let bygones be bygones. Come on in.

BRAD. Finally.

ERIC. One hundred and six.

PHILIP. Oh wait. We already have a hundred and five of you.

BRAD. A hundred and five?

PHILIP. That's all we're letting in each year. We may be allies but we still don't trust you.

ERIC. 1965.

(ding)

PHILIP. Policy change.

*(**BRAD** doesn't move.)*

PHILIP. Don't just stand there. Come on in.

BRAD. What do you want from me?

PHILIP. Just the password.

BRAD. Yellow Peril?

PHILIP. Welcome to the Land of the Free.

*(**ERIC** and **PHILIP** exit.)*

QING

*(**BRAD** sets up for the next part.)*

BRAD. In 1644, China is once again invaded. This time by the Manchus.

*(**PHILIP** enters dressed as a **JEW**. He wears peyos.)*

PHILIP. Shalom.

BRAD. The womanchus stay home to kvetch.

*(**ERIC** enters, dressed as a Jewish woman.)*

ERIC. You invade China, you don't write, you don't call. It's fine. Don't worry about me. It's okay. I'll sit in the dark.

*(**ERIC** exits.)*

PHILIP. *(to **BRAD**)* How do you do? I'm running for Emperor.

BRAD. So you're the Manchurian candidate.

PHILIP. I'm the only candidate. I win. I'm Emperor! Oy I'm filled with shpilkes. Okay first things first, where can we get good Chinese food?

BRAD. Everywhere.

PHILIP. What a country. Order something. I need a little nosh. Next, oy there are so many people here. It's like the Goldberg bar-mitzvah, which, by the by, must have cost the father a fortune. And his kid, not so bright, a bit of a schlemiel. Anyway, how do we tell you goyim from us?

BRAD. *(re: Philip's peyos)* Well, there's the hair.

PHILIP. The hair. Of course. You're a mensch. All the Chinese will shave their heads and grow long ponytails. Eh, "ponytails" sounds a little fey. Let's call them queues.

BRAD. I meant you all have those long sideburns...

PHILIP. You just went from mensch to pain in my tuckus. We're not shaving, so start growing your hair.

BRAD. And if we shave it off?

PHILIP. Death. Seems fair, right?

*(**BRAD** turns to the audience.)*

BRAD. I'd like to apologize to all of the Jewish-Americans in the audience for our grossly over-exaggerated portrayal of Jewish-Americans. You never invaded China, you never thought of invading China, and you had nothing to do with the Qing Dynasty.

*(**BRAD** exits.)*

PHILIP. Make fun of a Jew and he writes a scathing editorial in the local newspaper. But make fun of a Manchu, he'll kill you. Slow slice you.

*(**PHILIP** exits.)*

*(**ERIC** enters.)*

ERIC. We'll be covering all that is Jewish in our next show, Jews: The Fulshtendik Knish.

*(**ERIC** exits.)*

CHINESE CHECKERS

BRAD. Don't know what to give to your Chinese-Jewish friends for Hanukkah. This year, give them Chinese Checkers.[31] It's checkers played on the Star of David.

(**BRAD** *exits.*)

OPIUM - HU KNEW?

ERIC. After the United States declares its independence from England, Great Britain explores other shores.

(**ERIC** *and* **PHILIP** *enter dressed as British explorers.*)

(**BRAD** *enters.*)

ERIC. Cheerio.

BRAD. Coco Puff.

PHILIP. We have come from England. Very far away. On boat. Water.

ERIC. We have come to offer a proposition.

BRAD. That is a matter for the Minister of Propositions.

ERIC. Ah. And who is the Minister of Propositions?

BRAD. Yes.

ERIC. I said, who is the Minister of Propositions?

BRAD. Yes.

ERIC. The Minister of Propositions.

BRAD. Hu.

ERIC. There's a Minister of Propositions, yes?

BRAD. Yes.

ERIC. And who is the Minister of Propositions?

BRAD. Yes.

PHILIP. Allow me. Is it possible to offer the proposition to you?

BRAD. No.

PHILIP. Why not?

BRAD. He is no longer the Minister of Propositions.

---

[31] Chinese Checkers is not Chinese and Genghis Cohen did not invent it, as some historians believe. It's a German game called Stern-Halma. It was invented in the late 1800's. It has only been in the U.S. since 1928. It was first called Hop Ching Checkers then the name was changed to Chinese Checkers to make it sound more exotic.

PHILIP. Who isn't?

BRAD. No, Hu is.

PHILIP. Who is what?

BRAD. Hu is the Minister of Propositions.

PHILIP. We don't know the Minister of Propositions.

BRAD. He's new.

PHILIP. Who is?

BRAD. Yes.

PHILIP. Can you take the proposition to the Minister?

BRAD. No. They are no longer on speaking terms.

PHILIP. Who isn't?

BRAD. That's right. Hu staged a coup and overthrew Yu.

ERIC. I've been overthrown?

PHILIP. We don't know anything about a coup.

BRAD. It came from out of the blue.

PHILIP. What coup?

BRAD. Yu Hu.

ERIC & PHILIP. Cheerio.

BRAD. Booberry.

PHILIP. We have a proposition to make. May we speak to you?

BRAD. Yes. But only if a bribe is involved.

PHILIP. Ah ha! We need to offer you a bribe?

BRAD. Well he is the Minister of Bribes.

ERIC. Who is?

BRAD. No, Yu is.

PHILIP. It's you are.

BRAD. Yu became the Minister of Bribes after Hu overthrew Yu.

PHILIP. Perhaps if we started again.

ERIC. Cheerio.

BRAD. Frankenberry.

PHILIP. We have come from England. Very far away. On boat. Water.

ERIC. We have come to offer –

PHILIP. We have opium.

BRAD. Ooooo, opium. The Emperor says opium is illegal.

PHILIP. Piffleposh. We'll smuggle it in.

BRAD. We have tea.

PHILIP. It's a deal.

ERIC. Cheerio.

BRAD. Count Chocula

PHILIP. We have more opium.

BRAD. The emperor says all Chinese drug traffickers will be killed.

PHILIP. Twaddle-faddle.

BRAD. We have over a million opium addicts.

ERIC. Then you need more opium.

PHILIP. We have fourteen hundred tons.

BRAD. We have tea.

ERIC. And silk?

BRAD. And silk.

PHILIP. Cheerio.

BRAD. Tutti Frutti Twinkles.

ERIC. Why so blue?

BRAD. The Emperor says you English barbarians are smuggling in opium.

ERIC. He's right.

BRAD. So he dumped all of the Opium in the sea.

ERIC. Sacrilege.

PHILIP. This means war.

ERIC. Man the muskets and cannons.

BRAD. I have a stick.

> (**BRAD** *pulls out a stick.*)
>
> (**PHILIP** *breaks Brad's stick in two.*)

PHILIP. We win.

ERIC. I like Hong Kong.

PHILIP. It's lovely. We'll take it.

ERIC. I also like Christianity.

PHILIP. Amen. Release the Christian Missionaries.

ERIC. And pay us lots of money.

PHILIP. And stop calling us barbarians.

ERIC. And make opium legal.

BRAD. It seems a bit unequal.

ERIC. Of course it is. It's an unequal treaty.

BRAD. Take our tea, silk, and dignity.

PHILIP. I love being a large drug cartel.

ERIC. Here here.

(*GONG*)

(**ERIC** *and* **PHILIP** *exit.*)

BRAD. And speaking of opium, now is a good time to point out that Mount Everest, on the western border of China, is the highest mountain in the world.

(**BRAD** *exits.*)

BOXER REBELLION

(**PHILIP** *enters.*)

PHILIP. Welcome to China Square Garden. In the first heavy weight bout of 1900, in this corner, with a hatred for foreign devils, Christian missionaries, and Chinese converts, and with an extraordinary claim to be immune to bullets, the Righteous and Harmonious Fists, aka The Boxers!

(**ERIC** *enters.*)

ERIC. I'm taking the champ down. I'm taking him down to Chinatown!

PHILIP. Also in this corner, her name means "kindly and virtuous" but don't let the name fool you. She is evil incarnate, the Old Buddha, Tzu Hsi, The Empress Dowager!

(**BRAD** *enters.*)

BRAD. The white man is the devil and his knees don't bend.

PHILIP. And in this corner, the reigning champion and neighborhood bully, the United States, the United Kingdom, Italy, France, Austro-Hungary, Japan, Germany, and Russia…The Eight Nation Alliance!

(**PHILIP** *becomes the Alliance.*)

PHILIP. *(in a German accent)* I've got a message for you from Kaiser Wilhelm II: "Make the name 'German' remembered in China for a thousand years so that no Chinaman will ever again dare to even squint at a German."

ERIC. I'm gonna knock you out you big ugly kraut!

BRAD. Let the Boxer Rebellion begin!

    (ding!)

ERIC. Ain't no one can stop me. Not foreigners, not Christians, not bullets.

    *(**PHILIP** shoots **ERIC**.)*

ERIC. Okay, maybe bullets.

    *(**ERIC** dies.)*

PHILIP. *(German accent)* Winner and still reigning champion, the Eight Nation Alliance. And now I'm gonna pillage and plunder Peking.

BRAD. Always with the pillaging and plundering.

PHILIP. *(German accent)* It's what I do best.

BRAD. How much to make you leave?

PHILIP. *(German accent)* Three hundred thirty three million dollars.

BRAD. Okay.

PHILIP. And execute a bunch of your high ranking officials.

BRAD. I hate you.

PHILIP. *(German accent)* The feeling's mutual.

    (They break.)

PI & ICE CREAM

ERIC.
    THE CHINESE INVENTED ICE CREAM.
PHILIP.
    AND CALCULATED PI.
BRAD.
    AND THE FRENCH STOLE IT ALL AND CALLED IT PIE A LA MODE.

ALL.

>FRENCH PEOPLE SUCK.[32]

>(**ERIC** and **BRAD** exit.)

LAST EMPEROR

PHILIP. In December, 1908, at the ripe old age of two years and ten months, Pu Yi becomes the Emperor of China.

>(**BRAD** enters as Pu Yi.)

>(**ERIC** enters.)

ERIC. On October 10th, 1911, now really really tired of foreign rule, Chinese rebels cut off their queues and start a revolution.

>(**BRAD** cuts off his queue.)

BRAD. (singing)

>TALKIN' 'BOUT A REVOLUTION…

ERIC. The first gunshot is fired. October 10th becomes known as Double Tenth Day.

>(**ERIC** exits.)

BRAD. Pee Yu abdicates and becomes the Last Emperor. He marries Joan Chen and wins nine Academy Awards. His tutor, Peter O'Toole, returns to England and never wins an Oscar. Goodbye, Mr. Chips.

>(**BRAD** exits.)

>(**ERIC** enters.)

ERIC. Sun Yat-sen is elected president of the Republic of China and on January first, 1912, he becomes the father of modern China.

>(**PHILIP** enters.)

PHILIP. It's a boy! [33]

ERIC. But the sun soon sets on Sun Yat-sen.

PHILIP. So sad.

ERIC. Seriously.

---

[32] It's true.

[33] Philip always played Sun Yat-sen as Strom Thurmond. We don't know why. But it made us laugh.

(**PHILIP** *and* **ERIC** *exit.*)

BRAD. For the next several decades, lacking a leader, China plunges into chaos in what is known as the Warthog Period.

ERIC. (*offstage*) Warlord!

BRAD. Eventually two men vie for the leadership of China…

(**PHILIP** *enters.*)

PHILIP. Mao Zedong.

BRAD. And –

(**ERIC** *enters.*)

ERIC. Chiang Kai-shek.

(**BRAD** *exits.*)

PHILIP. Chiang.

ERIC. Mao.

PHILIP. Long time no see.[34]

ERIC. How are you?

PHILIP. Working hard. You?

ERIC. Hardly working. You look good.

PHILIP. I could lose twenty pounds.

ERIC. You were too thin before.

PHILIP. You're too kind.

(*pause*)

ERIC. Well I'm off, on the Road to Peking.

PHILIP. The Road to Peking? Me, too.

(*MUSIC*)

Song - *THE ROAD TO PEKING*

ERIC & PHILIP. (*singing*)
WE'RE OFF ON THE ROAD TO PEKING –

(**BRAD** *enters and motions to the booth to cut the music. The music stops.*)

BRAD. Telegram for Mr. Eric Hissom.

---

[34] Supposingly this saying comes from the Chinese expression" very long time-no see." I haven't been able to verify it but let's go ahead and believe it's true.

ERIC. I'm Eric Hissom.

(*He hands the telegram to* **ERIC** *and exits.*)

ERIC. (*reading*) It's from Bob Hope and Bing Crosby. Mr. Eric Hissom. Stop. Ba ba ba boom. Stop. Unable to grant rights to Road to Morocco. Stop. Cue Joesph Stalin. Stop.

PHILIP. Cue Joseph Stalin?

(**BRAD** *enters dressed as Joseph Stalin.*)

(*music*)

Song - STALIN

BRAD. (*singing*)
I'M AN EVIL DICTATOR
BUT I NEED A PARTNER
WORLD DOMINATION
IS GETTING MUCH HARDER
YOU'RE NOT MY TYPE, CHIANG
I HATE TO ADMIT IT
JUST LOOK AT MAO
BOY HE'S REALLY THE SHIT

ERIC.
HEY HEY HEY!

BRAD & PHILIP.
WE'LL PAINT THE WHOLE WORLD RED

ERIC.
I'LL GO TO TAIWAN INSTEAD

BRAD & PHILIP.
NOW WHO'S THE LOSER
WHAT A SCHLEMIEL
IT'S ÜBER HAPPY HOUR
CHEERS TO NEW WORLD SUPERPOWERS
EVIL ARCH VILLAINS DRINK TWO FOR ONE

(**ERIC** *exits.*)

PHILIP. Oh no, my water broke!

(**BRAD** *helps deliver the baby.*)

BRAD. Pushkin!

PHILIP. You did this to me, you blood thirsty son of a –

(**ERIC** *quickly enters.*)

ERIC. And on October first, 1949, Mao Zedong gives birth to the People's Republic of China.[35]

(They toast.)

ALL. Gom bui![36]

*(**ERIC** and **PHILIP** start to exit.)*

BRAD. Hey whoa, we totally skipped the Sinus - Asian-American War.

ERIC. The what?

BRAD. The Sinus - Asian-American War.

ERIC. Sino-Japanese War!

BRAD. Yeah, that's the one.

PHILIP. We cut it.

BRAD. You can't cut it.

ERIC. Okay, fine. On July 7th, 1937, Japan invaded China.

PHILIP. Bada-Bing. Moving on.

BRAD. Hey ho. We're skipping my song about the Rape of Nanking?

PHILIP. Rape is sort of a downer.

BRAD. It's a snappy little polka. Let me set the scene. A bunch of Asian-Americans invade China and in six weeks, the invading Asian-Americans kill three hundred thousand innocent Asian-Americans.

ERIC. Japanese! The Japanese kill three hundred thousand innocent Chinese!

BRAD. But one man comes to the rescue: Liam Neeson.

ERIC. What!?

BRAD. He's a Nazi, so you think he's bad guy, but he saves a bunch of Asian-American lives and turns out to be a good guy.

ERIC. That's Schindler's List!

---

[35] In the original production, Philip gave birth to a Chinese Flag. The flag was rigged in one of the cubes and Brad pulled it out from between Philip's legs. It really looked like Philip was giving birth to a flag. Okay, it only looked like that way to the blind guy with the obstructed-view seat, but it still looked pretty cool.

[36] It's Chinese for "Dry the Cup." Like "Skoal," "Salut," or "I'll have what the man on the floor is having!"

BRAD. It won an Oscar.

PHILIP. You're thinking of John Rabe!

BRAD. Who's John Rabe?

PHILIP. He's the Joseph Schindler of China.

ERIC. He was a Nazi living in China and he saved thousands of Chinese from being killed.

BRAD. Did he win an Oscar?

ERIC. He's not an actor!

BRAD. Neither is Nicholas Cage and he has one.[37]

ERIC. Can we just –

BRAD. Polka music, please.

ERIC & PHILIP. We cut the song!

BRAD. Then I'll have an inner monologue moment.

ERIC & PHILIP. A what!?

BRAD. Pensive music, please.

(music)

ERIC. Brad, what are you –? When did you record this?

PHILIP. Brad, are you mentally deficient? – Wait. Is this Rainbow Connection?

song - *NANKING SONG*

BRAD.
OH IS IT WRONG
TO SING A SONG
ABOUT THE RAPE OF NANKING
WHEN THE CHINESE
FELL TO THEIR KNEES
AND LOST EVERYTHING
AND THE WORLD SIMPLY STOOD BY
WHILE INNOCENT CHINESE DIED
OH IS IT WRONG
TO SING A SONG
A SONG ABOUT THAT

ERIC. Actually Brad, we voted two to one to cut the song.

PHILIP. Remember, we wrote our votes on paper so it would be a secret ballot?

---

[37] A shining example of the saying "life isn't fair."

BRAD.

> OH IS IT WRONG
> TO SING A SONG
> ABOUT THE NANKING MASSACRE
> A TRAGEDY
> IN HISTORY
> SOME SAY DID NOT OCCUR
> WHEN A PRIEST AND A NAZI
> AND A FEMALE MISSIONARY
> RISKED THEIR OWN LIVES
> TO SAVE THE LIVES
> OF STRANGERS
> IN DANGER
> OH IS IT WRONG
> TO SING A SONG
> A SONG ABOUT THAT

PHILIP. *(spoken)* Well, yeah Brad, it is because here's the big problem.

> *(singing)*

> YOU JUST USED THE WORDS
> RAPE AND MASSACRE
> WE CAN'T WAIT TO SEE WHAT'S NEXT
> YOU SHOULD HAVE BEEN MORE CIRCUMSPECT

BRAD.

> IS IT WRONG
> TO SING A SONG
> ABOUT MASS EXTERMINATION
> A PRACTICE WE
> ALL AGREE
> DEFIES EXPLANATION
> BUT IF WE'RE NOT TERRIFIED
> WHEN INNOCENT PEOPLE DIE
> THEN WE PRAY
> THERE'LL BE A DAY
> WE ALL WILL BE
> LIKE THAT NAZI
> AND THE PRIEST
> WHO CAME IN PEACE
> AND RISKED THEIR LIVES

TO SAVE THE LIVES
OF STRANGERS
IN DANGER
OH IS IT WRONG
TO SING A SONG
A SONG ABOUT THAT

(awkward pause)

ALL.
BANGKOK!

(MUSIC. Mayhem.)

BRAD. Dictator Mao.

PHILIP. Ixnay on the ictator day. Let's go with Chairman. Chairman's nice. It works for Sinatra. We need to catch up with the rest of the world. We need more steel, electricity, and coal. Let everyone in China know we're taking a great leap forward.

BRAD. That's a horrible idea.

PHILIP. Why?

BRAD. If everyone in China jumps at the same time it'll throw the world off its axis and hurl us into space.

PHILIP. That's an old wives tale.

BRAD. I have an old wife.

ERIC. So in 1958, China takes a great leap forward.

(They all jump and they all hurt themselves.)

*(***ERIC** exits.)*

BRAD. Chairman, the great leap forward is a catastrophic failure.

PHILIP. The earth is hurtling into space!? I thought it was an old wives tale. Who knew old wives tales were true? Oh why did I eat Pop-Rocks and soda for breakfast!? What have I done? I've destroyed life as we know it.

BRAD. No. The earth is fine. It's your plan. Good on paper. Not so good in practice. The steel is crap and millions of people are starving.

PHILIP. Oh…well at least we're not hurtling into space.

FAMINE

(**ERIC** *enters, dressed as an American housewife.*)

ERIC. Meanwhile, in the good old U. S. Of A.

(**PHILIP** *becomes a little girl.* **BRAD** *sits downstage left.*)

PHILIP. I don't want to eat my spinach.

ERIC. Eat your spinach. There are poor starving kids in China.

PHILIP. Name two.

ERIC. You want me to name two?

PHILIP. Yeah.

ERIC. Okay I will.

(**ERIC** *picks up a phone and makes a ringing sound.*)

PHILIP. Yeah like you know two kids in –

ERIC. I'll name two and then I'm gonna shove that spinach down your ungrateful throat.

(**BRAD** *picks up another phone.*)

BRAD. Yellow.

ERIC. China?

BRAD. Yeah.

ERIC. I need the names of two starving kids.

BRAD. We have about thirty million people who are starving to death.

ERIC. I just need two names. My brat child won't eat his food.

BRAD. You have food?

ERIC. Yeah. And my kid won't eat it.

BRAD. We'll eat it.

ERIC. I just need two names.

BRAD. We're all very hungry.

ERIC. Two names. That's it.

BRAD. If your son doesn't want his food maybe you could send it –

ERIC. Steve and Greg? That's great. Thank you.

(*He hangs up.*)

ERIC. Steve and Greg.

PHILIP. Those don't sound like Chinese names.

ERIC. That's what they said. So stop whining and eat your spinach.

PHILIP. But I don't want to eat my –

(**ERIC** *dumps the food off the plate.* **BRAD** *dies.*)

ERIC. There. You just killed Steve and Greg. Are you happy now?

(**PHILIP** *cries and runs offstage.* **ERIC** *exits.*)

CULTURAL REVOLUTION

BRAD. Meanwhile, back in China, killing 30 million people doesn't sit well with the Chinese, but Mao doesn't give up.

(**PHILIP** *enters.*)

PHILIP. I'm not giving up. I have another plan. A cultural revolution. The Communist Party is letting us down. Big surprise. We need radical change. We need to destroy the Four Olds; Old Culture, Old Habits, Old Ideas, and Old Man River. Tell all the students to stop going to school and join the Red Guard. This is a war on bourgeois liberalism and culture. To rebel is justified.

BRAD. Okay.

(**BRAD** *starts to leave.*)

PHILIP. Oh and sell my Little Red Book.

(**PHILIP** *tosses a book to* **BRAD**. **BRAD** *exits.*)

(**ERIC** *enters.*)

ERIC. Chairman, your revolution is once again a catastrophic disaster. Everything has been destroyed and nearly thirty million people have been killed.

PHILIP. Thirty million again? Ooo, that's not gonna look good on my resume.

ERIC. On the bright side, you've out Hitlered Hitler. He only killed twelve million.

PHILIP. There's that.

ERIC. On the brighter side, your Little Red Book is selling like hotcakes. Nine hundred million in print. Second only to the Bible.

PHILIP. Take that J.K. Rowling!

(**PHILIP** *and* **ERIC** *exits.*)

(**BRAD** *enters.*)

NIXON

("Star Trek"-ish music)

BRAD. In 1972, at the height of the Cold War, the United States and the Klingon Empire prepare for a peace summit. President Nixon bristles at the thought of negotiating with a sworn enemy.

(**PHILIP** *enters as Nixon.*)

PHILIP. Pat, pour me a scotch.

BRAD. But Secretary of State Spock tells him "There is an old Vulcan proverb: Only Nixon could go to China."

PHILIP. Oh very well.

(**ERIC** *enters.*)

ERIC. In a sign of goodwill, Chairman Mao sends Nixon a gift: two panda bears. Ling-Ling and Hsing-Hsing.

(**ERIC** *exits.*)

PHILIP. I don't trust anything named Hsing-Hsing.

(yelling offstage)

Send Mao two musk oxen. Their horns look like bad toupees. He'll think that's hilarious. And bug their horns.

(**PHILIP** *exits, but sticks his head back on stage*)

PHILIP. I am not a crook.

(and exits.)

TIANANMEN SQUARE

BRAD. And then in 1989, the entire world casts its eyes upon a student demonstration in China.

song -GATE OF HEAVENLY PEACE

ERIC.

> IN THE SPRING
> OF '89
> HU YAOBANG
> PASSED AWAY
> AND THEY CAME
> FROM MILES AROUND
> TO THE GATE OF HEAVENLY PEACE

BRAD.

> AKA
> TIN MAN SQUARE

PHILIP.

> TIANANMEN SQUARE
> YOU IDIOT

ERIC.

> THE STUDENTS PRAYED
> FOR HIS SOUL
> AND THEY PRAYED FOR
> DEMOCRACY
> AND THEY PRAYED
> THE LIGHT WOULD SHINE
> ON THE GATE OF HEAVENLY PEACE

ALL.

> THE GROUND CRACKED OPEN AND THE SKY GREW
> DARK
> CAME A RUMBLING ACROSS THE LAND
> THE DEVIL ROSE UP AND HE DECLARED
> I'M GONNA CRUSH YOUR FAITH INTO THE GROUND
> I'M GONNA CRUSH YOUR FAITH INTO THE GROUND
> I'M GONNA CRUSH YOUR FAITH INTO THE GROUND
> AT THE GATE OF HEAVENLY PEACE

PHILIP.

> THERE WAS A MAN
> DENG XIAOPING
> HE WAS SMALL
> FOUR FOOT FIVE

BRAD & ERIC.

> HOBBIT SMALL.

PHILIP.

> HE WAS ONE OF
> EIGHT ELDERS
> HE WAS A HARD LINING MAN

BRAD.

> LITTLE DENG
> WAS HOPPING MAD
> DEMONSTRATORS
> EVERYWHERE
> SO HE SAID

PHILIP.

> I'VE HAD ENOUGH

BRAD.

> AND DECLARED
> MARITAL LAW

ERIC & PHILIP.

> MARTIAL LAW!

ALL.

> THE GROUND CRACKED OPEN AND THE SKY GREW
> DARK
> CAME A RUMBLING ACROSS THE LAND
> THE DEVIL ROSE UP AND HE DECLARED
> I'M GONNA CRUSH YOUR FAITH INTO THE GROUND
> I'M GONNA CRUSH YOUR FAITH INTO THE GROUND
> I'M GONNA CRUSH YOUR FAITH INTO THE GROUND
> AT THE GATE OF HEAVENLY PEACE

ERIC.

> THE STUDENTS LAUGHED
> IN SATAN'S FACE
> SAID OLD MAN
> WE'RE NOT AFRAID
> BRING YOUR FIRE
> AND YOUR BRIMSTONE, TOO
> WE'RE GONNA LET FREEDOM RING
> ERIC AND PHILIP EXIT.

BRAD.

> THE STAGE IS SET
> BATTLE LINES DRAWN
> GONNA FIGHT TO THE DEATH

> (**PHILIP** *enters. He wears a cardboard tank and an army helmet.* **ERIC** *enters. He carries a protest sign.*)

BRAD.
> IN THE MORNING
> OF JUNE 3RD
> NOTHING HAPPENED AND EVERYONE WENT HOME
>
> (**BRAD** *continues to sing.*)

BRAD. *(singing)*
> EVERYONE WENT HOME. NOTHING HAPPENED.
> EVERYONE ATE SOME RICE. MAYBE SOME CHICKEN.
> BECAUSE NOTHING HAPPENED. NOTHING WAS
> WRONG.[38]

ERIC & PHILIP. Brad! No. Wait. Stop. Brad.

> *(The music stops.)*

BRAD. What?

ERIC. Nothing happens!?

BRAD. No.

ERIC. Are you crazy?

PHILIP. I mow down thousands of people. I crush their faith. Crush their bones. Tank Guy tries to stop me. I mow him down. I mow everyone down.

ERIC. Yu Dongyue throws ink on Mao's portrait and gets imprisoned for seventeen years.

BRAD. Well I don't know where you're getting your information but I went to China and searched the internet for Tiananmen Square and came up with a big goose egg.

PHILIP. You couldn't find anything because of the Great Firewall of China.

BRAD. The Great Wall is on fire?

PHILIP. Internet censorship. There are some things the Chinese don't need to know. Democracy, freedom of speech, equality, police brutality –

ERIC. Philip!

PHILIP. Let me talk. The Dalai Lama, Tibet, the Taiwanese government, the fact that Chinese weapons –

ERIC. Philip!

PHILIP. No no. This is important. The fact that Chinese weapon are fighting the war in Darfur, BBC Sports –

---

[38] Brad always adlibbed something here. "They went to KFC. Had some chicken. They love their KFC. Yum Yum." Things like that.

ERIC. BBC Sports?

PHILIP. Very subversive. And if the Chinese discover these things exist, they'll no longer be a ruthless killing machine.

ERIC. They're not a ruthless killing machine. Just stick to the script.

PHILIP. You want me to stick to the script? Okay, I'll stick to the script. After "nothing happens" on June 3rd and 4th of 1989, China slowly takes over the world.

ERIC. No no no. They don't take over the world!

PHILIP. Can you hear them coming?

ERIC. Philip –

PHILIP. They're taking over the world.

ERIC. They're not –

PHILIP. They're taking over the world! They're coming, Eric! They're coming! Are you blind? They're poisoning our pets, our toothpaste, they're lacing our kid's toys with lead paint. They're putting formaldehyde in our pajamas. Two kids burst into flames while wearing those pajamas! They're killing us while we sleep!

ERIC. That does it!!!

*(**ERIC** throws down his protest sign. He and **PHILIP** square off and they inadvertently reenact the Tank Guy moment.)*

ERIC. We are trying to do a show about how wonderful China is –

*(**ERIC** lunges for **PHILIP**.)*

*(**PHILIP** backs up.)*

PHILIP. Beep, beep beep.

ERIC. And you have ruined it with your sick Sinophobic ways!

(They run offstage.)

(crash)

PHILIP. I'm just preparing people!

ERIC. Prepare to die!

(more crashes)

(**ERIC** *runs on. His fingers are caught in a Chinese finger trap.*)

ERIC. Ah ah!! Get this off me!

(**PHILIP** *enters.*)

PHILIP. It's amazing what they can do with paper!

ERIC. You need help. Serious serious help.

(*The struggle continues.*)

ERIC. You've ruined it! You've ruined the show! Ruined it!

PHILIP. Good!

ERIC. Fine!

PHILIP. Fine!

(**ERIC** *and* **PHILIP** *go to opposite sides of the stage. They all stand in silence for a few seconds.*)

(*They all stand in silence for a few seconds.*)

(*Then* **BRAD** *walks center stage.*)

LINUS SPEECH

BRAD. Lights, please.

(*A spotlight shines on* **BRAD**.)

BRAD. Philip, I understand your fears. The unknown can be very scary. We know very little about the Chinese. But they're not war mongers. Far from it. Most of them want what we want: a happy family, a good job, a home, freedom. I'm sure a lot of people think Americans are war mongers. Can you blame them? I mean, look at us. Hello, Iraq. But most of us don't want war. We're very peaceful people. And so are the Chinese.

And Eric, we can't gloss over the negatives and pretend the Chinese are without faults. Yes, their government is corrupt. Whose isn't? Have you been to Washington, DC lately?

The Chinese have brought the world countless contributions: cultural, religious, scientific. They brought us fireworks, paper money, and a place for Jews to eat on Christmas Day. The Chinese aren't all bad, Philip. And they aren't all good, Eric. They're like you and me. Good and bad. Strong and weak. Yin and Yang. And that's what China – The Whole Enchilada means to me, Charlie Brown.

(They stare at **BRAD** *for a few seconds.)*

ERIC. Brad, that's really insightful.

BRAD. Oh! Shih Tzus come from China.

PHILIP. Which reminds me, China also invented toilet paper.

BRAD. That was a crappy segue.

ERIC. Okay. Let's not waste time. There's a whole lot more.

PHILIP. Ah, grasshopper. To give everything of something is to bring an end to it. China is ever changing, ever growing, ever elusive.

ERIC. But –

PHILIP. Snatch the pebble from my hand.

*(***PHILIP*** reaches in his pocket and pulls out a rock. But before he can open his hand,* **ERIC** *opens his hand.* **ERIC** *already has the rock.* **PHILIP** *opens his hand. His hand is empty.)*

PHILIP. Wow! I guess it's time to go.

BRAD. How about an exit song?

(They all look at each other.)

ALL. Hit it.

(Music starts.)

PHILIP.
THEY'VE GOT THE GREATEST WALL, THE LARGEST MALL,
A GRAND CANAL, THEY DRINK TSINGTAO
THEY GAMBLE ON AN ISLAND CALLED MACAO.

ERIC.
THERE'S HENAN, HUNAN, CANTON, TAIWAN,
WUHAN, XI'AN, SZECHUAN, JINAN,
AND CELESTIAL MOUNTAINS TIAN SHAN

BRAD.

> THERE'S HIROSHIMA AND TOSHIBA SONY, SAKE, AND
> MOUNT FUJIYOKOHAMA, HONDA, AND A GEISHA
> THERE'S TOKYO, KYOTO, AND SAPPORO
> NAGASAKI, KAWASAKI

ERIC & PHILIP.

> NO YOU IGNORAMUS THAT'S JAPAN!

BRAD. Oh.

ALL.

> IT'S CHINA
> NOT TOSTADA, EMPANADAS, MICHELADA,
> CHIMICHANGA.
> CHINA

PHILIP.

> WE HOPE YOU DIDN'T MIND-A THERE WAS REALLY
> NO PLOTLINE-A

ALL.

> YES IT'S CHINA.

BRAD.

> I MUST BE GOING BLIND-A CAUSE I MISSED THE
> CONCUBINA.

PHILIP.

> DID YOU KNOW IN LIECHTENSTEIN THERE IS VERY
> LITTLE CRIME-A

ERIC.

> BOY IT'S GETTING HARD TO FINDA ANY MORE
> WORDS THAT WILL RHYME-A

BRAD.

> AND WE STILL WENT ALL THIS TIME-A AND WE
> DIDN'T USE VAGINA

ALL.

> YOU CAN'T SPELL ENCHILADA WITHOUT C-H-I-N-A!
> YES IT'S CHINA, THE WHOLE ENCHILADA!
>
> *(BLACKOUT)*

The End

ACT 1	PHILIP	BRAD	ERIC
Base	Black Shirt Black Pants Black Sneakers Black & Gold Chinese Jacket Chinese Skull Cap	Black Shirt Black Pants Black Sneakers Red & Gold Chinese Jacket Chinese Skull Cap	Black Shirt Black Pants Black Sneakers Maroon & Gold Chinese Jacket Chinese Skull Cap
Pre-Show Announcement	Long Blue Chinese Robe Wild Chinese Hat	Coolie Hat Coke Glasses Buck Teeth	Base
DISCLAIMER	Base	Base	Base
CHINA - THE WHOLE ENCHILADA	Base	Base	Base
Overview		Base	Base
The Beginning	Pope Robe Pope Hat	Headlamp	Base
Act 1	PHILIP	BRAD	ERIC
PEKING MAN	Pope Robe Pope Hat	Caveman Pelt Caveman Wig	Base
SHANG (Oracle Bone)	Base Base Hat	Base Base Hat	Base
Zhou	Base	Base Little Bamboo Hat Little Bowtie	Base Big Bamboo Hat Big Bowtie
Lord of the Rings		Long White Robe Long Blonde Wig Elf Ears	
First Emperor	Cowboy Hat	Base Base Hat	Base Base Hat
CHOPSTICKS	Base	Base	Base
Han Dynasty		Obi Wan Robe	Base
Wang Mang	Groucho Glasses with Red Eyebrows		Groucho Glasses with Red Eyebrows
Carrington Dynasty	Base	Base	Base
LOTUS SHOES (Tang Dynasty)	Black Dress Female Wig	Pink Dress Little Girl's Wig	Purple Dress Female Wig
KHAN-KHAN	Long Black Robe Khan Triangle Hat Purple Vest Mustache	Red & Brown Full Chest Exposing Shirt Gold Chain Gold Wrist Cuffs	Black Leather Vest Khan Hat Mustache

Act 2	PHILIP	BRAD	ERIC
Mooncake Festival	Long Black Robe Purple Vest Khan Triangle Hat	Base	Base
Ming Dynasty	Red Ming the Merciless Robe Huge Ming the Merciless Collar Black Ming the Merciless Skull Cap	Flash Gordon Shirt (Underdressed) Blonde Wig (Flash Gordon) Long Red Robe (Fu) Short Red Robe (Fu, Over Long Robe) Black and Red Chinese Hat (Fu) Mustache (Fu)	Dale Arden Wig
EVIL IS A YELLOW FACE	Same as Ming	Same as Fu Manchu Dog Ears (Hong Kong Phooey)	Dale Arden Wig Gold Bikini Top (Dale Arden) White Jacket (Chan) White Hat (Chan) Mustache (Chan)
Inventions	White Lab Coat Short Gray Wig		Green Vest Green Jacket White Lacy Collar Tri-Corner Hat with Wig Ben Franklin Glasses
Yellow Peril	Uncle Sam American Flag Jacket	Gray Jacket Base Hat	Chef Hat Irish Hat
Qing Dynasty	Long Black Robe Hat with Peyos	Base	Jewish Mom Glasses Jewish Mom Wig
Chinese Checkers		Base	
Opium Wars	Khaki Shirt British Pith Helmet	Base Base Hat	Khaki Shirt British Pith Helmet
Boxer Rebellion	Announcer Shirt Kaiser Helmet	Long Red Robe Black Dowager Hat Chinese Fan	Boxing Robe Boxing Gloves
PI AND ICE CREAM	Same as Boxer Rebellion	Same as Boxer Rebellion	Same as Boxer Rebellion
Last Emperor	Gray Jacket	Base Base Hat with Removable Queue	Gray Jacket
STALIN	Gray Jacket	Bushy Stalin Mustache Gray Jacket	Gray Jacket
Sino-Japanese War	Gray Jacket	Base Base Hat	Base
NANKING SONG	Gray Jacket	Base	Base
Great Leap Forward	Gray Jacket	Base Base Hat	Base

Act 2	PHILIP	BRAD	ERIC
Famine	Little Girl Pigtails	Base	Red, White and Blue Apron Female Wig
Cultural Revolution	Gray Jacket	Base	Base
Nixon	Blue Sport Coat	Base	Base
GATE OF HEAVENLY PEACE	Red Choir Robe	Red Choir Robe	Red Choir Robe
FINALE	Base	Base	Base

PROPS

Hookah
Bible
Headlamp
Large Egg
Troll Doll
Test tube herbs & holder
Cup
Magic 8 Ball
Book
Large Box of Whoppers
Groucho Glasses with Red Eyebrows (2)
Large La Choy/Chung King Can
Tang
Lotus shoes
Duct tape
Hong Kong Phooey Dog Ears

Kite
China bowl
Turkey baster
Knitting needles
Bowl of spaghetti
Abacus
Compass
Constitution of the United States
(Need not be the original)
Declaration of Independence
Must be the original)
Yellow Pillow
Small Suitcase
Bell
Chinese Checkers
Stick

Chinese Fans
Gun
Boxing gloves
Telegram
Large Chinese Flag
Plate
Spinach
Mao's Little Red Book
Tank
Chinese Finger Cuffs
Crash Box

www.ingramcontent.com/pod-product-compliance
Lightning Source LLC
Chambersburg PA
CBHW072150130726
47909CB00004BB/1475